D1565999

THE
STATIONMASTER

THE
STATIONMASTER

Jiro Asada
TRANSLATED BY TERRY GALLAGHER

VIZ MEDIA
SAN FRANCISCO

Poppoya © 2000 by Jiro Asada
All rights reserved.
First published in Japan in 2000 by SHUEISHA Inc., Tokyo.

English translation © VIZ Media, LLC

Cover art © 2009 Mark Roberts Elliot
Designed by Sam Elzway

Published by
VIZ Media, LLC
295 Bay St.
San Francisco, CA 94133

www.viz.com

Asada, Jiro, 1951-
[Poppoya. English]
The stationmaster / Jiro Asada ; translated by Terry Gallagher.
    p. cm.
"First published in Japan in 2000 by SHUEISHA Inc.,
Tokyo."
ISBN-13: 978-1-4215-2763-5
ISBN-10: 1-4215-2763-4
I. Gallagher, Terry, 1956- II. Title. PL845.S27A613 2009
895.6'35--dc22

                            2009003007

Printed in the U.S.A.
First printing, April 2009

STORIES

The
Stationmaster

From the platform of Biyoro Station, the single-track Horomai line paralleled the main line for a short distance until it left town. The resort express, with its big glass windows, would get a good long look at the single diesel car of the Kiha 12 as the express slowly overtook it.

Perhaps it was just a quirk of the schedule, or maybe it was a special show arranged for the enjoyment of the skiers from the city, but as usual, the passengers on the express train clustered at the windows to see the solitary diesel painted the vermilion red that was the emblem of the old Japan National Railways. When the Horomai line finally veered to the left around the big curve headed for the pass, the big glass windowpanes of the express lit up with a sudden burst of flashbulbs.

The 18:35 Kiha 12 was the last of just three trains that traveled to Horomai each day.

"What do they get so excited about? Not worth taking pictures of, eh, Gramps?" The young engineer turned his head to gaze at the express as it moved farther away across the field of snow. He looked up at Senji, who was standing in the number two spot.

"Don't get smart. The Kiha 12 is like a museum piece. People come from all over the country just to see this train."

"Oh yeah? Then why are they going to shut down the line?"

"You know why. Not enough freight traffic density, profits, stuff like that."

The young engineer stood his thumb up on his shoulder and waved. The train had but a single car and not a soul in it. Just the green seats lined up starkly beneath the dim fluorescent lights.

"Not words I ever thought I'd hear from the stationmaster of Biyoro Central Station."

"What do you mean?"

"I mean, Gramps, who the hell cares about the 'freight traffic density' on the Horomai line? I've been working this line for four years now, and every year, as soon as school lets out, this is what it's like. So I'm just wondering why the hell they decide to shut it down all of a sudden."

"Who knows? That's just the way it is. The only reason it's lasted this long is its past performance. You were born and raised in Horomai, you know how much livelier it used to be around here."

Horomai, at the end of the line, was one of just a handful of coal mining towns in Hokkaido and had been active since the Meiji period in the late nineteenth century. Six stations lined up along the 21.6-kilometer stretch of tracks. The line was a buzz of activity, with D51 steam locomotives running coal cars back and forth. Now, morning, noon, and night, just a solitary diesel car made the round trip, its only passengers high school students. The stations along the way were no longer staffed. Ten years had passed since the mine was shut down.

"They say old man Otomatsu at Horomai Station is going to retire this year. Maybe that's the reason."

"Don't talk like you know what the big executives are thinking. You think anybody down in Sapporo cares about stuff like that?"

The Kiha 12 made a brief stop at the deserted North Biyoro Station as if paying a courtesy call.

"Hey, what are we going to do if this snow doesn't stop? It'll pile up all over everything."

"Don't you worry about that. Let's move it along!"

Still standing in the assistant's spot, Senji seemed suddenly in a hurry, and his voice rose. "All clear ahead!" he hollered as the diesel began to glide once again across the fields of snow.

Senji tugged at the detachable white collar of his uniform jacket and continued their conversation. "We're not just talking about other people here. Otomatsu may be retiring this year, but next year it's my turn."

"Yeah, Gramps, I heard you're going to be some big cheese at the station building."

"Who told you that?"

"Everybody in Biyoro knows. The new station building is going to be finished next year and you're going to get some big important management job there."

"What a load of nonsense. It's just a maybe at this point. Can't really see myself getting all dressed up in a suit and tie like those department store employees from the mainland, smiling and bowing to all the customers."

"I hear you. Once a railroad man, always a railroad man. Just like those steam locomotive engineers in the old days—to the end of the line!"

The young engineer raised his left hand and tugged down on an imaginary rope, imitating the sound of an old train whistle: "Toot, to-oot!"

Senji turned his gaze slowly over the engineer's cabin of the Kiha 12, its walls covered in many layers of ancient paint. His eyes landed on the brass plate that read HOKKAIDO RAILWAY CO. When Japan Railways had been broken up and privatized, each of the new regional companies had gotten a similar name. But the character for "railway" (鉄道) that the owners of the Hokkaido Railway Co. adopted differed slightly from what the other railway companies used (鉄道).

Using the characters for "lose" (失) and "money" (金) in the name of their company seemed a bad omen for a railway system with so many money-losing lines. So the Hokkaido Railway officials settled on the not very common character 鐵 instead of 鉄. A small difference only a true railway man would notice.

"So, what's going to happen to me? I mean, what if they say to me, 'From now on you'll be driving trains on the main line'?"

"What do you mean?"

"I don't know anything about those fancy new trains they have on the main line. Or worse, they tell me I gotta work in a kiosk or cook ramen or something. I couldn't take that."

"Don't worry about that. If you can drive this old rattle-trap you can drive anything, even a *shinkansen*. Be thankful you're young."

"The bullet train? I've never driven any train over fifty kilometers an hour. Just thinking about it gives me the shivers."

Senji wiped the windshield with his cotton work gloves.

The train started up a gentle slope. Ridges of earth ran close along either side. At the far end of each of the many short tunnels the train passed through, the snow was a little deeper.

"What do you think, Gramps? Tomorrow they'll have to send out the Russell snowplow."

Staring at the tracks ahead of them illuminated by the train's lamp, Senji had the sensation that they were entering some strange, mythical country. He propped his elbow on the switchboard and gazed steadily ahead at the play of light and shadow on the snowy landscape.

"Once we get to Horomai you should head straight back. If you wait and get stuck on the way, there won't be any-body at any of the stations to help you out, this close to New Year's."

The engineer looked longingly at the big sake bottle at Senji's feet.

"I thought maybe I'd spend the night in Horomai."

"Don't be stupid. What if there's somebody waiting to take the last train back?"

"Ha! Now who's being stupid."

The train stopped at another station between the mountains. There were no passengers waiting. Not a single light shone in any of the dilapidated buildings around the station.

"You don't want to spend New Year's at Otomatsu's. What do we two old men have to talk about but the old days? Think about it. You want to end up drunk and sentimental like us? Huh?"

"Nah, I was just kidding, Gramps. Not my style. Moving! All clear!"

"You've got the voice down, all right."

"Got it from Otomatsu."

After what seemed like a long time, they reached the headwaters of the frozen river and saw the lights of Horomai. On its back the town bore the dark shadows of the slag heap.

"Blow the whistle. We're five minutes behind schedule, and Otomatsu will be waiting out on the platform."

The old whistle of the Kiha 12 echoed through the hills, as if lamenting what little was left of its life.

Through the round mouth of the tunnel, Horomai Station hove into view. Amid the derelict buildings of the old coal mine, under the shadow of the monstrous conveyor, the station at the end of the line was gleaming white.

Senji and the engineer pointed to the signal with its wooden crosspiece and spoke in unison. Searchlights illuminated the brick platform. Once upon a time, this freight yard was packed with engines and gondola cars, but now it was just a field of snow.

"Would you get a look at that, Gramps? It's like a fairy tale."

The wheels rumbled along the tracks. Snow falling all around him, on the platform at the end of the line stood the stationmaster, holding his lantern high.

"Look at him standing out there, even though we're five minutes late and it must be twenty below."

The snow piling up on the shoulders of his thick JNR overcoat, his deep blue uniform cap fastened under his chin, Otomatsu stood ramrod straight at the end of the platform. He stretched himself even taller in the cold and, with his finger in the cotton work glove, pointed smartly down the line where the train was approaching.

"He's looking good, Otomatsu is. Like a picture."

"Hey, don't be cheeky. At your age, you can't just call him 'Otomatsu' like you've been best friends forever. He's 'Stationmaster' to you. Just look at him. Now that's a railroad man. And not just any old JR stationmaster that you could strip the uniform off of, stuff in a suit, and make into some old terminal building executive."

"Just looking at him makes me want to cry."

The engineer blew the whistle once more and applied the brake. The Kiha 12 came to a halt at the platform, its diesel engine still roaring.

Otomatsu came walking down the platform to the train. The thin layer of snow that crunched under his boots was no more than what had fallen in the five minutes of the train's delay.

"Ah, Oto-san, I feel cold just looking at you. Sorry to keep you waiting," Senji said as he alighted from the train, smiling.

"Don't mention it. Happy New Year!"

"Same to you, Happy New Year! I meant to spend New Year's Eve with you, but my son Hideo came home with his new baby."

"What's that? Hideo's a daddy? Well, that must mean you're a granddad. Your first grandchild. Must be cute!"

"You bet your life he's cute!"

The words had scarcely left his lips when Senji covered his mouth with his gloved hand, as if he had said something that would pain Otomatsu.

"I invited Hideo to come up with me to visit you. But tomorrow is his first day at his new job. You understand."

"Don't worry about it. Hideo must be busy with his new responsibilities. Section chief at Sapporo headquarters! Tell him not to worry about me."

"I'll make sure he comes up to see you by springtime, hat in hand. When he first joined the company, wasn't he the big man, saying the Horomai line would never die as long as he had any say in the matter. What can I say? We couldn't do it. As you well know."

Senji removed his hat and bowed his bald head.

"Senji, knock it off. The stationmaster of Biyoro Central Station shouldn't be bowing his head to me. It's embarrassing."

Brushing right past Senji, Otomatsu peered into the engineer's cabin. "Welcome! Come on into the station and warm yourself up before you have to head back out again."

With a glance at the back of Senji's lowered head, the engineer said, "With the snow falling like this I better head straight back. Thanks anyway, Stationmaster."

"I see. 'Stationmaster,' eh? Senji must have scolded you. There's no need to be so formal. It's a touchy subject. I'm 'master' of none."

So saying, Otomatsu pulled out a little flag from behind his back. Bending his tall body, which was thin like a crane's, he tapped Senji on the back.

"Senji, you've put on weight."

"Is that so?" Senji said, finally lifting his head. "I ate too much holiday food. By the way, my wife sent this for you."

"Thanks, but she didn't have to do that. Now it feels like New Year's. Go on ahead inside. I'll be in as soon as I see this train on its way."

While Otomatsu prepared for the departure of the last train of the day, Senji crossed the tracks and entered the station house.

Horomai Station had been built before World War II, and it had hardly changed a bit in all those years. It was a striking building with a big waiting room, a high ceiling, fat tobacco-colored rafters, and the beautiful, triangular panes of stained glass just under the eaves. High up on the wall above the ticket-taker's booth there still hung the old JNR symbol, a driving wheel, like something left behind and forgotten. All the benches were antiques, shiny and black.

Senji wondered to himself if there were no way to save even the building. Weary from standing the whole trip, he sat down on a bench and warmed his hands at the oil stove.

The train whistle's blast broke the silence.

"Sorry to keep you waiting. Have a look. The Daruma restaurant across the way closed down."

Otomatsu carried the scent of snow into the station, furling his hand-flag as he pointed to the little shop.

"Is that a fact. What's happened to the old lady?"

Just one general store had stuck it out all those years in front of the station, but now its roof sagged under the snow and its lights were all dark.

"Her son bought an apartment in Biyoro. The old lady was over seventy, and there was nothing left to keep her here. Before long I'll have to start selling cigarettes and newspapers right here."

"Don't talk nonsense, Otomatsu. All by yourself you're going to sell the tickets, do the cleaning and track maintenance, and on top of that you want to run a kiosk too? Nonsense!"

"Listen here. There are still a hundred or more households in Horomai. Now, maybe we're all old, but we still like to read our newspapers every day."

From the office came the sound of an old *enka* song. Just outside the station, the shadow of the old slag heap bore down like a weight. Senji lit a cigarette.

"Say, we should start our New Year's celebration. Hideo bought a bottle of local sake from Sapporo for me to bring you."

"You shouldn't have gone to all that trouble. You even brought New Year's food. Ever since my wife died, New Year's has been nothing special around here."

"How many years has it been now since Shizue died?"

"How many years? Just the year before last. But it feels like it's been a decade already."

"Otomatsu. You must miss her."

"Not particularly. I have plenty of company here in the village. I don't have to miss her. Now, I'm going to damp down the stove and we can go inside."

Before they started drinking, there was something Senji had to say.

"I came to tell you, Otomatsu, that next spring I'm going to move over to a job at the station building."

"Is that a fact? I'm glad to hear it."

"And I was wondering whether you wouldn't like to move down to Biyoro too. It's a twelve-story building with glass elevators. It's a joint venture of a Tokyo department store and JR. I might have a little pull I could use for you."

"Well, I wouldn't want you to use up your pull on my account."

Senji shut his mouth, regretting his use of that particular expression.

"I appreciate it, but I think I'll pass."

"Why, Otomatsu?"

"Hell, I'm scared even to get on an escalator. We might both be just railroad men, but I never climbed the ladder to be stationmaster of Biyoro Central Station the way you did. That's a big difference."

"But Otomatsu! You know your way around machines."

"Not hardly. The only thing I understand is railroading.

Never finished school. Everything I know I learned with my body, poking around with a shovel in my hand. To any of those fancy Tokyo department store employees, I would be like some kind of foreigner."

Into the lull in the conversation crept the awesome quiet of the snowy night.

"So, Senji, are you saying Hideo is down there in Sapporo doing what he can for me?"

"Nothing of the sort. I mean, he graduated from Hokkaido University, and he passed the management exam, so he's bound to make something of a career, but he's not so high up in railroad management that he can have a say in what lines are going to close or stay open."

"Sure, I understand."

The snow on Otomatsu's shoulders stayed frozen, stubbornly refusing to melt. Senji brushed it off and felt himself at a loss for words.

Otomatsu asked, "How's the wife?"

"Doesn't change at all. Plump as ever."

All of a sudden, Senji had an unpleasant recollection. In his mind, he saw Otomatsu in the hospital morgue the night his wife died, silent, his head hung low. To this day, Senji's wife resented that Otomatsu had not been at his wife's side to witness her death with his own eyes. She still thought Otomatsu unfeeling.

Though they had sent many messages that her condition was critical, he had waited for the last signal at Horomai Station and had come to Biyoro on the last train. They called and called, but in the end it was only Senji's wife who was at Shizue's side when she died. She could not forgive Otomatsu for not being there.

Then as now, as Otomatsu stood by Shizue's pillow and hung his head, his uniform coat was covered in a patchwork of ice and snow. Senji's wife wondered aloud why he didn't cry, and he mumbled back at her, "I'm a railroad man. We don't cry about family."

Senji had gazed at Otomatsu, who gripped the hem of his coat but shed not a tear. He could vividly recall the sound of the D51 on the rails and smell the diesel smoke.

"Say, Sen," Otomatsu said, doffing his cap and holding it over the stove. It was a navy blue JNR cap with a dull red band and the badge of the JNR train wheel symbol. Senji felt somewhat ashamed of his own blue cap.

"What is it?"

"Forget about me, but what's going to happen to the Kiha?"

"Hmmm. The Kiha 12s were manufactured in 1952, back when we two were stoking the fires on the old D51s."

"So you're saying it's headed for scrap."

"It's worked hard, it has."

Senji could still clearly remember the first day the brand-new Kiha 12 had pulled into Horomai Station. He was brushing the chassis of the D51 with a bundle of coarse rope. Otomatsu was in the tender, shoveling coal. Miners and villagers crowded the tracks. When the sparkling Kiha 12 emerged from the darkness of the tunnel, the voices of the people rose up in an enthusiastic cheer.

"Hey, Sen, would you get a look at that! It's the new steam engine, the Kiha 12!" Up in the tender, Otomatsu waved the shovel. The shouts of *Banzai!* did not stop until the stationmaster took the driving staff in hand.

"I was just a boy shoveling coal, and now I'm ready to retire. I suppose it would be cruel to ask that the train work even harder than us humans."

"Otomatsu, that train might just be the very last Kiha 12 still running anywhere in Japan. If we play our cards right it might end up in a museum or some kind of railroad park. Somebody will take good care of it, don't you worry."

"I wouldn't mind being displayed in some museum myself."

And at that they both smiled.

"Well, let's dig in to these New Year's treats."

The platform lights were out, and the station waiting room was lit just by the glow of the snow outside.

"What's this? Somebody forgot something..."

On one of the benches that lined the walls sat a plastic doll with her arms outstretched.

"Yeah, there was someone playing there until just a little while ago. She must have gone home."

In the darkness, Otomatsu ran to the vestibule and looked out in front of the station.

"I haven't seen that kind of Kewpie doll in years. It's really old-fashioned. You think a passenger left it behind?"

"No, it was a little girl I've never seen before. She was playing here for the longest time."

"What do you mean? How could there be a little girl here *you've* never seen before?"

"Maybe she's here for a New Year's visit. Maybe she came in a car. She was cute as a button, with a bright red backpack."

"Backpack, you say?"

"She said she would be starting elementary school this spring, so her dad bought her a pack for her books. She was so cute, and she made a fuss over me. 'Look, it's the station-master!' And she stuck right with me and wouldn't leave me alone."

"She could tell you like kids."

Otomatsu had no children. He lived in a tiny apartment at the back of the station: two rooms, each measuring six tatami mats, with a kitchen area in one. There was a small family altar with a picture of his father wearing his railway uniform and one of his wife when she was very young.

Senji lit a stick of incense and gazed at the photographs for a while.

"Otomatsu, there's no picture of your little girl."

"That's because she was only two months old when she died."

"What was her name?"

"We called her Yukko. Short for Yukiko, 'child of the snow,' because the first snow of the winter fell on the day she was born, November 10. Don't you remember? You were talking about fixing her up with Hideo."

"I remember now. Hideo was in junior high school. I kidded him about marrying her, and he looked at me like I was nuts. He never did even hold her."

The two of them sat at a low, round table with bottles and cups of cold sake between them. When they turned the radio off, they could hear a faint sound of water dripping.

"It may seem a bit strange, but I still keep track of Yukko's age. She would be seventeen now if she had lived."

"You were already middle-aged when she was born."

"I was forty-three and my wife was thirty-eight when we were blessed with her. What a shame." The note of sadness in Otomatsu's voice was out of character.

The unerring clock on the big post was pointing straight to midnight when Otomatsu Sato sensed there was someone at the passenger gate.

"Stationmaster! Stationmaster!" A soft voice was calling to Otomatsu through a gap in the acrylic window over the ticket counter.

"Who's there at this time of night? Is there an emergency? Is somebody ill?"

Otomatsu stepped quietly around Senji, who was fast asleep with the quilt pulled up over his head. He opened the curtain that covered the window, and there stood a girl with a red scarf around her neck and her elbows propped on the sill of the ticket window.

This girl seemed bigger than the one from the previous evening, but her smooth-lidded eyes were very like those of the other girl.

"Did you come for the lost doll?"

The girl nodded.

Otomatsu was in his nightclothes. He pulled on a padded cotton house jacket as he went out into the waiting room. He noticed that at some point it had stopped snowing, and from the vestibule window a stripe of moonlight splashed across the floor.

There was a faint roaring sound.

"Are you her older sister?"

He handed over the plastic doll, and the girl smiled and nodded.

"She's done nothing but cry since she lost her doll."

"That's nice of you to come fetch it. I haven't seen the two of you before. Where are you from?"

He was sure the girls were from the city, what with their fine, pale features.

"Our name is Sato. By the shrine."

"Is that so? Sato is such a common name, everybody around here is named Sato. Even my name is Sato. By the shrine, you say? The oil salesman?"

The girl shook her head.

"Isa's granddaughters? Torao's?"

The girl shook her head again, as if she didn't want to answer. Perhaps, in this village full of old people, she was tired of having to explain everything.

"We came to visit Grandpa. Because it's New Year's."

Otomatsu decided he should stop prying.

"It's dangerous to be walking around outside by yourself. There may not be bears around here, but you could get stuck in the snow or slide down an embankment, and then you'd be in trouble. I'll walk you home. Wait right here."

"No, no, don't bother. It's just over there. And the moon is bright."

There was no nonsense about her. She knew how to speak

her mind.

"How old are you?"

"I'm twelve."

"Junior high school? A little small for your age?"

"I'm still in sixth grade. Junior high is next year. Station-master…" she said haltingly, stamping her feet against the cold.

"You have to pee? The toilets are outside, to the right. Wait a minute, I'll turn on the lights."

He opened the office door quietly and flipped a switch on the panel, bathing the snowy platform in a dim, flickering light.

"I'm a little scared. Will you stay with me, Stationmaster?"

"Sure, sure. I'll be right here."

Again she hesitated and took Otomatsu's hand.

"There's nothing to be afraid of. That's right."

Grasping her small hand, Otomatsu felt a certain sadness wash over him. The girl from yesterday evening and now this girl reminded him of Yukko. Could this be because his life as he now knew it would end in just three more months?

If only they hadn't let Yukko catch that chill, she might be here like this today, all grown up, and he might be accompanying her outside on her nightly visits to the toilet. But she had been born in this remote village with no doctor, sleeping in the room behind the office where the drafts blew right in through the gaps in the sliding doors. When he thought it could be said that his job had killed his daughter, the pain of it overwhelmed him.

As he waited outside the restroom for the girl to emerge again, Otomatsu gazed vacantly across at the opposite platform.

One day, seventeen years ago, in the middle of a blizzard, he had put his wife on a train on that very platform, their daughter wrapped up in her arms. As always, he himself had given the hand signals and the verbal checks as the train left the station. Later that evening, he boarded a train, wrapped Yukko's cold body in the very same blanket, and came home again.

"Are you waving your little flag to welcome back your dead daughter?" That was what his wife, huddled on the platform, clutching Yukko's body, had said to him.

What had he said back to her?

"What am I supposed to do? I'm just a railroad man. There's nothing I can do. If I don't wave the flag on the platform in a blizzard like this how will the Kiha know where it's going? I have to throw the switch. School will be out, and the kids will be coming home."

"Your child has come home too. She's come home as cold as the snow itself."

That was the one and only time Shizue had ever raised her voice to Otomatsu.

He would never forget the staggering weight of the tiny body in his arms, heavier even than the ice-bound track switch.

Another voice awoke from deep in his memory.

"Uncle! Yukko, is she dead?" It was Hideo's voice. He had dropped his canvas knapsack, wedged himself between Shizue and Otomatsu, and snatched Yukko's body from Otomatsu's petrified arms.

"Oh my little Yukko, I'm so sorry. You were going to be my bride. Aunt Shizue, I'm so sorry. Don't scold Uncle Otomatsu. He's waving the flag for all of us! Okay, Aunt Shizue?"

Shuttering his bitter memories behind the breast of his padded cotton jacket, Otomatsu thrust each of his hands into the opposite sleeve and hung his head.

In the spring, if he were no longer a railroad man, then it would be okay to cry, he thought to himself.

"Thank you, Stationmaster."

The girl came out of the restroom, and he handed her a little can of coffee he had been warming inside his jacket.

"Have a drink of this before you go," he said. "You're cute. Your mother must be a beauty. So who are your parents exactly?"

"I'll drink half, and the other half is for you."

"No, I don't need any. It's all for you," Otomatsu said.

All his life, Otomatsu had kept an eye on the children of the village as they grew up. When their time came, all had gone off to some big city somewhere, but he did not forget a single face. Nothing could be sweeter than those sweet scenes of families and children, even other people's children, seeing them grow and change. What greater pleasure could there be? When he looked at them, he could not help but wonder what his own child would be doing now, had she lived.

At some point he had stopped going to Biyoro because it pained him to see girls close to the age his daughter would have been. Just wandering through the shops of the city he found himself looking at things that would be suitable for a girl of Yukko's age. Once he had picked up a red backpack and thought about it. Another time he actually bought a scarf and sweater, but he couldn't bring them home, so he had given them away to a child he happened to pass.

The young girl on the platform finished the can of coffee and tugged at his sleeve. She gestured to him that he should bend down.

"What is it?" he asked.

As he bent forward so that his face was near hers, the girl very deliberately grabbed him by the neck. She squirted coffee from her mouth to his, and it dribbled down his chin.

"Oh! You surprised me! What's all this about?"

The girl jumped up on the platform, fell down on her backside, and laughed.

"Stationmaster! I kissed you!"

"What a thing to do! You're a mischievous one, you are!"

"I'll be back tomorrow! Bye-bye!"

"Bye-bye! Be careful going home. Take your time, and be

careful of the snow banks on the roadside!"

She went back out through the station gate and spun around several times, as if she were dancing.

"I told you not to run!"

By the time Otomatsu reached the waiting room, the girl was nowhere to be seen. The room was flooded with moonlight, and the plaster walls had a magic lantern pattern from the multi-colored stained-glass panes. On the far side of the squeaky door was a sleepy-faced Senji.

"What's up, Otomatsu? It's still dark. Just midnight. We've hardly slept at all."

Senji looked again at the clock on the post and yawned a big yawn.

"Remember the girl from yesterday, the one who forgot her doll? Well, her sister came in to get it. What's this? She left it behind again!"

There on the bench sat the doll.

"She'll be back for it."

"You can bet on it. Even if I wanted to take it to her, I don't know what house she's in."

Senji looked past the ticket gate to the moonlit platform beyond. Something about Otomatsu was odd.

"Otomatsu, I think you must have been dreaming. Girls that age aren't out walking around by themselves this late at night."

"Well, she has a pretty face, but she's one restless kid, I'm telling you. Must be from Sapporo or Asahikawa or someplace like that. City kids are all night owls, you know."

"But it's the middle of the night. Must have been the Woman of the Snow."

"Huh?"

"Nothing...nothing."

Otomatsu picked up the doll, went into the office, and sat down at the desk. He pulled out a blank form and began to fill out a passenger report.

Senji went back on the morning train. That afternoon, Otomatsu received a phone call from the head office in Sapporo. When he heard where the call was from, Otomatsu stood straight and motionless, at attention, and then he heard an old familiar voice.

"Happy New Year! It's Hideo. How've you been?"

"Ah, Hideo! Oh my—sorry, I shouldn't be addressing a headquarters section chief so casually. If you're looking for your father, he took the first train back to Biyoro this morning."

"I wanted to go up there with him, but this is my first day at my new job."

"Don't worry about that. It seems I'm causing you a lot of trouble. Thanks to you, I'll be able to retire the same time they close down the Horomai line. The fates are frowning on us old railroad men. I was talking to your dad about that."

Silence at the other end of the line. Otomatsu pictured Hideo sitting at his desk at Sapporo headquarters hanging his head, and he chuckled.

"Otomatsu, I'm sorry. I just finished your paperwork, and it just didn't feel right to send it off to you like that without a word. So I'm calling to apologize."

"Don't worry about it. Your dad told me you've been trying hard to convince the higher-ups. I'm sure that can't be good for your own career."

"Actually, I haven't been able to accomplish a thing. It was all my dad. He came down to headquarters and tried to speak to the executives. Every year he collected ten thousand signatures in Biyoro on petitions to save the line."

"You don't say. He never mentioned that. I didn't know."

"Whenever he had a day off, he would change out of his stationmaster's uniform and put on regular work clothes, and from morning to night he would stand in the underground shopping center. It may seem strange for a son to be saying these kinds of things about his father, but I understand what you may be feeling, so I'm asking you, Otomatsu, not to feel bitter toward my dad about the line closure. I'm sorry, but it just wasn't within my power to stop it."

"Not at all. I'm sorry if you had to squander your time, Section Chief."

Again silence at the far end of the line. Just the sound of Hideo's breathing.

"Otomatsu, I am grateful to you from the bottom of my heart."

"Now don't go saying such silly things. It's embarrassing."

"No, I mean it. The only reason I'm able to be here right now, doing what I'm doing, is that you were there all the time, rain or snow, to see us off at Horomai Station and welcome us home again. I don't quite know how to say this, but your encouragement meant a lot to me."

"That alone wasn't enough to get you into Hokkaido University. And it was you who passed the management exam."

"That's what I'm trying to say, but it's not coming out right. None of us, not me, not the ones who went down to Tokyo, none of us will ever forget you."

"Oh…is that so? It's too much. I don't know if I can take any more."

When he'd set down the receiver, Otomatsu felt that all his strength had drained from him. The full weight of a half-century rested on his shoulders. He gripped the desk with both hands, and for a moment he was unable to either sit or stand on his own.

In the afternoon it snowed some more, heavily enough to obscure even the silhouette of the slag heap. Silence settled over the world. In the quiet Otomatsu heard a buzzing in his ears he might have mistaken for the hum of the rails. He bent his white, close-cropped head into his hands.

At the sound of tapping at the ticket window, Otomatsu lifted his head. A teenage girl, her hair in braids, was brushing the snow from her gabardine coat.

"Hello, Mr. Stationmaster!"

Her polite bow reminded him of someone. Then he realized this must be an older sister of the two girls who had come yesterday, and instantly his heart lightened.

"You, you must be the older sister…"

"You recognized me?" Holding her mittens to her cheeks, she smiled.

"What's not to recognize? Your voice, your face—just the same as the other two girls."

"I have to apologize about yesterday. I'm so sorry, Mr. Stationmaster."

"Nothing to be sorry about. It was all just good fun. Come on inside for a minute. It's drafty out there."

She looked around the waiting room in wonder and gave a little gasp of surprise at the stout rafters and the old-fashioned stained glass. Her profile was radiantly beautiful.

"Home for the holidays?"

"That's right," she said, swinging her braids like rope and looking over her shoulder.

Otomatsu thought he had it finally figured out. "You three must be Yoshie's daughters, over at Enmyo-ji Temple."

"Hmm?" she asked, confused, then smiled again. "Is that who I look like?"

"You look just like Yoshie when she was in high school. Ah, that's a load off my mind. All this time I've been wondering whose kids you are. I've been wondering who was the right age to have girls as cute as the three of you. And then I thought, 'Yoshie Sato!' She was always a good student. I think she was the student body president at Biyoro High School. Come on inside. Now that I know who you are, I can't let you go home without a bowl of New Year's sweet bean soup."

"Don't mind if I do," she said as she slid open the office

door. She removed her coat, folded it, and held out her hands toward the stove. Otomatsu was surprised to see she was wearing a sailor-suit school uniform, navy blue with white piping.

"That uniform you're wearing, it looks just like the old Biyoro High School uniform. Now they all wear blazers, but in that uniform you really do look just like Yoshie."

"Lots of Hokkaido schools have uniforms like this."

Otomatsu could remember when the station waiting room had bustled with high school students in those days before the mine finally closed. Every morning there must have been at least thirty of them, all in their navy uniforms with the gold buttons. With the train waiting to depart, Otomatsu would call out the signals while his wife treated the students to sweet red bean soup and *amazake* to drink.

"I always make this on January 1, but I can never finish it. Eat up!"

She perched on the edge of the raised, tatami-covered eating area and took the bowl of sweet bean soup in both hands.

"So the priest at Enmyo-ji Temple has three cute grandchildren home for New Year's. Bet he's happy."

The girl warmed her fingers on the bowl and looked into the room.

"Wow, it sure is nice and tidy here."

"It's just the way I do things. Daytime there's nothing else to do."

Otomatsu thought to himself that the priest over at Enmyo-ji must talk a lot. It wasn't good to have people know too much about the life of a sixty-year-old widower. It was embarrassing.

The girl's lips were like the petals of a flower. She pursed them to sip her soup. From time to time she fixed her eyes on Otomatsu.

"What is it? Never seen a rural stationmaster before?"

"No, that's not it. It's just, your uniform, it's so sweet!"

"This you mean?" he asked, tugging at the sleeves of his old-fashioned double-breasted jacket. "I have a newer one, but I've never gotten used to it. I like this one better."

Outside the window it had started to snow.

"Look, it's snowing again. You shouldn't waste any time. It's blowing sideways."

He heard no reply, and when he looked again, he saw she had gone into the next room and was examining his collection of railroad memorabilia.

"Wow, you have a number plate from a D51!"

"You interested in old railroad junk?"

"This would fetch three hundred thousand yen! You have a lot of great stuff. Metal destination signs, all kinds of things…"

"You're really nuts about this stuff, aren't you?"

"I'm in the railroad club at my high school. I'm the only girl."

"Well, that's different, all right."

Otomatsu was happy. Once or twice a year, some city kid crazy about trains would show up at his station. Talking to these kids about the good old days of the JNR was Otomatsu's greatest pleasure. Sometimes their conversation went on so long Otomatsu would end up putting them up for the night. But those kids never came back for a second visit. No matter how interested they were in railroads, a local line with a single train going back and forth was just too lonesome for them.

Otomatsu did his best to explain everything. The metal destination signs, number plates from steam engines, all kinds of old parts and ancient tickets. He even had an old-fashioned date stamp, the kind you'd never see at any other station anymore.

"Why don't you pick something to take home with you? Anything you like. Before long—" What he started to say was, *Before long, this spring in fact, this line's going to close down anyway.*

"But I have no money."

"Who said anything about money? Don't be shy, pick something."

"You really mean it? Anything? Even this D51 plate?"

"Sure, anything at all. The old man at Enmyo-ji has done a lot for me over the years. This household's always been in his congregation, in a way."

When the girl had finished her soup, she disappeared into the kitchen with her bowl, quite at home.

"Don't bother with that. You don't have to do that."

But she turned her sailor-suited back to him, standing like a lily in the dim light of the kitchen, and turned on the water.

"Tell me more stories about the railroad," she said.

Otomatsu thought to himself, *That old priest, he could have called me on the phone.* The more he thought, though, it occurred to him that this may have been the priest's way of being kind. If this girl hadn't shown up, Otomatsu might have started drinking in the middle of the day and then napped until the evening train arrived.

Perhaps they had even enlisted Senji in their plot, just trying to make him feel better, Otomatsu thought to himself.

That day in Horomai the snow blew so hard both time and place were completely obscured. The old station building was buried in pure white, no sound, no light.

The girl was no chatterbox, but she listened intently to each of the old stationmaster's memories. Every silly thing, every proud thing he had done in the past fifty years—Otomatsu dug up one old story after another, so many that he wondered at himself.

Somewhere deep within the breast of that old uniform, these memories lay like layers of sediment: the smell of the trains' diesel smoke, the feeling of coal cinders. With each event he recalled, Otomatsu's being grew lighter.

He remembered the days of Japan's economic boom. A coal mine disaster, when the station house filled with the bodies of dead miners. Labor demonstrations, when the riot police had come. And he remembered the mines that were closed, one by one, like lights being put out.

Asked, however, what had been the most difficult thing, Otomatsu kept to himself the story of his daughter's death. That was private. For Otomatsu Sato, the most awful thing in his life had been the death of his daughter, and the second most awful thing the death of his wife. What he said, though, was that as a railroad man, the saddest thing was seeing off all the young people who left each year to find jobs.

"Kids two or three years younger than you, crying as they left the village. But it wouldn't do for me to cry, no matter how sad it made me feel. It wasn't easy, but I had to tell those kids to get out there and do their best, pat them on the shoulder and tell them to smile. And then I'd stand at the end of the platform at attention, long after I could no longer see the train, until I couldn't even hear the whistle blowing anymore."

He remembered that on one occasion, Senji had been the engineer driving the train full of job-seeking young people. That time, the train's whistle blew for a long, long time.

Railroad men never cried, they just blew their whistles. They didn't shake their fists, they waved their flags. They never shouted out in anger but put that energy into the voice they used for calling out the signals. That was how railroad men made it through their troubles.

"All this talking, where has the time gone? It's time for the last train. When I'm done here I'll see you home to the temple. Take care you don't catch cold. Here, put this on."

Otomatsu put the quilted cotton house jacket over her shoulders and stepped down into the office. He draped his coat over his own shoulders, fastened the chinstrap of his cap, raised his lantern, and exited the station building. The clock on the post struck seven.

After quickly shoveling away the snow, Otomatsu took up his post at the end of the platform. A circle of light appeared in the tunnel. The train that emerged from the veils of snow was the powerful DD15 Russell snowplow.

Watching the Russell come driving toward him, blasting the snow before it, pulling the empty train behind, Otomatsu felt sorrow well up from the bottom of his heart. *That train has listened to my foolish pride to the very end.* He had no right to accept any pension, any retirement bonus, he thought.

In his right hand he held the lantern high. With his left, he pointed his finger down the track, and he called out the signals in a wrung-out voice.

The young engineer stepped down from the train along with a linesman Otomatsu knew very well.

"Some snow we're having here today, eh, Mit-chan? You have time for a break, don't you? Have some sweet bean soup!"

"Thanks a lot, Otomatsu. I appreciate it. But we have to turn right around and get this plow back down to the main line. I just have time to take a leak. Oh, by the way, we brought you something. It's from all the railroad workers in the district."

The linesman handed him a beautiful basket of fruit.

"What's that all about? I still have another three months. You're too early for my retirement party."

"No, you've got it wrong. This is for your family altar."

The two railway men's shoulders shivered as they headed for the restroom.

After seeing off the snowplow train, Otomatsu picked up his present and headed back inside the station building. The linesman had casually dropped that phrase about "all the railroad workers in the district," but Otomatsu knew instinctively what was going on. The old hands had not failed to remember the anniversary of Yukko's death. The linesman had handed him the gift as casually as he had handed over the tablet ring, and all Otomatsu could do was to silently accept this token of their affection.

Otomatsu stood in the wood-framed ticket gate, removed his snow-covered hat, and bowed his head as the sound of the rails faded off into the distant gloom of the snow.

There was no way he could ever eat this whole magnificent basket of fruit, so he made up his mind to offer it to Enmyo-ji Temple.

"Well, young lady, it's time to go. You can take the D51 plate with you. That's right. And don't forget the doll!"

He opened the door to the steamy office and stopped in his tracks.

For an instant Otomatsu thought he was seeing his late wife seated cozily at the table.

"My darling!" he said. But it wasn't so. The red quilted jacket was the one she'd always worn, but the back turned toward him belonged to the girl.

"What is it, Stationmaster? Look, I made you something to eat."

"But, but this is a feast! You made all this?"

"Sorry, but I thought you wouldn't mind if I looked to see what was in the fridge."

"Not at all. You made all this in the few minutes I was outside?"

On the small low table was a meal for two: dried fish, scrambled eggs, stewed vegetables.

"You mind if I use these?"

Smiling, the girl picked up a bowl and chopsticks.

"Those belonged to my late wife, but I don't mind. Go right ahead. I am just amazed. You're a really good cook!"

"The electric rice cooker takes too long, so I made the rice over the fire. I hope it's cooked enough."

"You must be some kind of magician, I think, to be able to whip this together from the leftovers in the fridge. I feel like I'm under some sort of spell. Well, this looks good. Let's eat!"

"I always dreamed of marrying a railroad man, so I knew I would have to be able to cook a meal quickly, just like this."

"Well, you passed the test with flying colors."

Otomatsu brought the miso soup to his lips, and a strange feeling came over him. It tasted just like his wife used to make.

"You like it?"

"I'm overwhelmed."

"Why is that?"

If Yukko had lived and learned to make miso soup from her mother, they would have eaten together just like this, he thought to himself. This would have been their regular evening meal after he saw off the last train.

He set down his chopsticks and knelt formally.

"All my life I've followed my own path, and in the end it cost the lives of my daughter and my wife. But now, here you are, doing these nice things for me. I couldn't be happier than I am right now."

"Really?"

"I really mean it. I could die at any time and be completely satisfied."

The phone rang. Otomatsu, in his slippers, went to the office to answer it.

"Hello. Ah, priest! Happy New Year! Your granddaughter's been here the whole time. She's quite a beauty. She made dinner for the two of us."

But the priest over at Enmyo-ji had not called to check on a granddaughter who was late coming home. After exchanging a few pleasantries, the priest asked what Otomatsu meant to do about this year's memorial service for his daughter.

When Otomatsu hung up, he couldn't turn around. His

shoulders sagged, and he slumped into the chair. He could still hear the priest's words echoing in his ears.

"What's up with you, Otomatsu? You must be going crazy. Yoshie didn't come back here for New Year's, and neither did anybody else."

Otomatsu picked up the plastic doll from the desk, and with his finger he toyed with the lace around its waist.

"Do things like this really happen?"

He could see the girl's reflection in the window.

"You, you lied to me."

The falling snow brushed against the frozen windowpane.

"I didn't want to frighten you. I'm sorry."

"Frighten me? What father would be afraid of his own daughter?"

"I'm sorry, Father."

He looked up at the ceiling, tears streaming down his cheeks.

"Since last night, you've been showing me what you would have looked like growing up. Last night you were here with your backpack, showing me how smart you looked. And then, in the middle of the night, you were a little older. When you came back again you were wearing that Biyoro High School uniform, so we've covered the whole seventeen years."

Her voice was as quiet as the snow piling up outside. "Dad, you've had nothing but trouble your whole life. I died before I was ever able to be a real daughter to you. That's why I came back."

Otomatsu hugged the doll to his chest.

"Now I remember. Your mother cried and cried when she put this doll in your coffin with you."

"That's right. And I've taken good care of it. You bought it for me in Biyoro. And Mom knitted her dress."

"You know, the day you died, I shoveled snow off the platform. And in that day's log, I sat at this very desk and wrote, 'Nothing unusual.'"

"But Dad, you're a railroad man. There was nothing you could do about it. All that stuff, I don't hold it against you."

Otomatsu turned in his chair and looked at her. Yukko shrugged her shoulders in the red quilted jacket and smiled a sad smile.

"Let's finish eating. And then you can take a bath. You can sleep here tonight, Yukko."

In the day's log, Otomatsu once again wrote, "Nothing unusual."

That night, once the snow had stopped, a brilliant, silvery full moon shone over the slag mountain of Horomai.

"Wow, I've never seen this many people on the Horomai line. The train is full!"

The young engineer picked up the conductor's bag and walked the length of the platform, peering in at the seats of the Kiha 12.

"Of course, you fool! It isn't every day we lose a stationmaster who has served for forty-five years. This is not the funeral of your average everyday dignitary!"

"I have to admit, though, Otomatsu, I mean, the *Horomai stationmaster* looked good. I hope I look that good when my time comes. Look, there at the edge of the platform is the snow bank where he collapsed, with his flags in his hand and his whistle in his mouth."

"Knock it off. I don't want to hear you talking like that."

Before Senji entered the engineer's compartment, he stood at the end of the platform and stomped down the snow. Otomatsu had collapsed the day after Senji had come home from that lonesome New Year's night they spent together. The crew of the day's first train, a Russell snowplow, had found his body face down in the snow.

"You drove that night, didn't you?"

"That's right. In the Russell, with Michio from the engine section."

"Did anything seem strange to you? About Otomatsu I mean."

"Not really. He seemed fine to me. Maybe he should have seen a doctor or something. Wait a minute, it's coming back."

"What's that?"

"I remember now. Michio and I visited the outhouse. And I thought to myself I should call my girlfriend, so I went to the office to use the phone. And there I saw that the table was set. For two."

"There was a meal on the table for two?"

"It was weird. I couldn't imagine Otomatsu eating with anyone."

"Well, it's not impossible. He might have had someone over for dinner. It's not that strange."

"No, it wasn't like that. When Otomatsu's wife was alive, I ate with them plenty of times. I know what his wife's rice bowl looked like. And that night it was there on the table, and his wife's red quilted jacket was out, lying on the *zabuton* cushion. I didn't mean to be nosy, but it gave me the creeps."

"You're just thinking too much. Didn't you say the village children often came to visit him?"

"I think it was the Grim Reaper himself who came to visit him. Came to get him."

"Don't talk like an idiot. Who ever heard of the Grim Reaper coming dressed up like a cute little girl? He wasn't himself. His wife died. The line was going to be closed, he was going to retire. That would be too much for anybody."

"You know, the priest from Enmyo-ji Temple was just here. He said Otomatsu had been acting a bit strange lately."

Senji looked all around at the mountains that ringed Horomai. After the snowfall, the sky was a flawless blue, like a painted landscape, and made a perfect complement to the JNR vermilion of the Kiha train.

"He died peacefully. Waiting on the snowy platform for the first train of the day, collapsed from a stroke. —Say, let me drive the train. I should be the one to drive Otomatsu."

"You want to drive the train?"

"No need to fear. I drove D51s for ten years and Kihas for ten years after that. I'm a better driver than you. Look here, let me have the controls!"

Senji gave the engineer a push and wedged himself into the narrow driver's seat of the Kiha 12.

"If they know I'm driving, they'll all get scared. Lower the shades! Is Otomatsu on board?"

Otomatsu's coffin was in the aisle of the train car, between the seats filled with uniformed railroad men.

"Yes, he's on board. This was a brilliant idea, to transport him to the Biyoro crematorium in the Kiha. It's dramatic, it's memorable. I can't believe I still have another three months of driving this empty train back and forth, and without him there."

"Michio will stay here starting tonight as provisional stationmaster."

"You're kidding! Scares me just to think about it."

Senji opened the ancient leather satchel and pulled out mementos of Otomatsu. He pulled on the cotton gloves, put the old JNR cap on his head, and tightened the chinstrap. The familiar oily scent of railway men cheered him up.

His throat tight, Senji called out the signals: "All clear! We're moving!"

He pointed his finger at the crossbar signal in front of the train, the bright glare of the afternoon in his eyes.

In front of the station was the hand-operated rail switch, the freight yard full of rusty rails and wooden railroad ties with their spikes. The landscape of Horomai, which had not changed a bit in ages and ages, was slowly starting to move.

Senji felt the hard surface of the old steam engine beneath his hands, and memories of his days of steel with Otomatsu filled his mind.

"Otomatsu, watch this! You and I are going to chant the prayer of the dead for this old rattletrap."

"Stop it, Gramps, I'm gonna lose it!" The engineer, standing in the assistant driver's spot, sniffled.

No matter how the world changes, we are railroad men. We make that silly "Toot-toot" sound in that silly high voice, and we wave our steel arms as we head straight down the line. We aren't allowed to cry like normal people, Senji thought to himself, biting his lip.

As the train entered the tunnel, the powerful roar of the wheels filled his ears.

"Gramps, just listen to the sound of this train. She's really crowing! Sure the bullet train has its own sound, and the North Star has its own special whistle too, but the sound of the Kiha just makes me want to cry. I can't explain it, but my eyes fill up just hearing that sound."

"Hang on there. Just hold that thought. Just hang on. We're still railroad men."

Each time Senji felt his own eyes fill with tears, he sat up straight and sounded the Kiha's whistle, loud and long.

Love
Letter

As the hired manager of a shady video store and other such ventures, he would sometimes get snitched on and spend a night in jail, but even if the prosecutor was in a really foul mood and things ended up in court, the worst he ever got was a fine. The money was good for the risk involved, and if once in a blue moon he got arrested, he got bonus pay for that. With the extra dough he got for the once or twice a year he ended up in the slammer, it was a lot better than being a lousy bartender.

All he really had to do was make sure he kept his mouth shut. For a man like Goro Takano, who had spent twenty years earning his keep in Kabuki-cho and knew everything there was to know about the place, from the bitter to the sweet, this was a dream job.

One day, perhaps because he had just been released from the Shinjuku police station, he caught the scent of spring in that urban landscape that knows no seasons.

This time he had spent ten days in the lockup, and for a while he had even been worried, but in the end his trial had been postponed and he had been allowed to go. He couldn't remember a word of the lecture the prosecutor and the detective had given him, but he remembered that sense of the changing season.

He always thought that when he turned forty he would

clean up his life and go straight. He had thought this even in his late twenties, and after he stopped tending bar he had gone on to the obligatory stint as a general bagman. Later he ran a porno shop and then a game store, and before he knew it eight years had gone by. In the usual order of things, next he would be a curbside tout or the manager of a rip-off bar, but right now he was at a loose end. He had always been a pretty smart guy, but never all that tough, and somehow he had not quite moved up to that next job.

It was nearly sundown but still hot and sticky, and in the crowded street Goro took off his good leather jacket. Now that he was nearly forty, it was not that he couldn't do the tout job if he wanted to. But this leather jacket and jeans, his favorite outfit for years, just weren't going to cut it. He would have to wear a suit and tie, to show himself as someone people could trust. But just the thought that that's what he would have to do, every day, was more than he could bear. And on top of that, it would cost money.

Just ten days ago, the porno shop had been raided. Both the sign outside and the interior needed to be changed so it could get right back in business. He wanted to see who his replacement was as store manager, and he stuck his eye to a gap around the peephole in the door to try to get a glimpse. He saw a bored teenager sitting at the counter watching a video. Nobody he knew.

He sensed someone behind him, and then something tapped him on the head.

"What're you up to there, Goro?"

It was one of the vice detectives from the Shinjuku police station, where he had just been to say goodbye.

"You tailing me or something? Leave me alone!"

"Not at all. I haven't got time to be tailing a chump like you," the detective said as he grabbed on to Goro, pulled him away from the door, and kept moving.

"I forgot to tell you something important, so I came after

you in the patrol car, but I got here ahead of you because you were on foot and taking your sweet time. I knew you'd be headed here."

"What do you mean, something important?"

It's not like he was a real gangster or anything, so reviled that they would arrest him at the jailhouse door right after letting him go. If this was about some other investigation, Goro made up his mind to keep his mouth zipped.

"You're a real pain in the ass, you know that? Why don't you just quit this small-time crap and become a real gangster? Then the lines would be clearly drawn."

"I'll never be a gangster. I'm too scared of the mob cops. Not like you."

The detective wrapped one overcoated arm around Goro's neck and turned the corner into an alley.

"Smoke?"

"I quit smoking. Bad for my health."

Laughing through his nose, the detective lit up his own cigarette. He stood shielding Goro from the eyes of passersby, spewing smoke.

"It's about your wife. She's dead."

Goro stood bewildered, unable to absorb this news.

"Listen to me, Goro. Your woman. Your wife."

"Is...is that so?" He had no idea what else to say. His "wife"—that could only mean the foreign woman who had come to Japan to work. A yakuza friend of his had asked him last summer to marry her by putting her name in his family register.

"Yeah, we had a call this morning from the police over in Chiba. What was it they said exactly..." the detective said, leafing through his notebook. "Hakuran. Nice name. Yeah, says here Hakuran Takano got sick and died, and somebody should come pick up the body. I swear, I don't know why things like this have to involve the police. Well, now I've told you, so you'd best be on your way."

The detective wrote down the phone number of the

station in Chiba and the contact person's name and handed the piece of paper to Goro, and then turned his back as if to say he had nothing more to do with this.

"You mean I...I have to go there?"

"You kidding? I don't care if this was some kind of sham marriage or what, it's none of my business. Listen, I gave you the info. You're going to have to wipe your own butt on this one."

"It's got nothing to do with me either."

"Listen, if you can't take care of this, I'm just going to have to pass it along to the organized crime detectives. If this turns into a real investigation, my bet is you're a dead man. Wouldn't that be right, Goro? My sincere sympathies." With those words, the detective slipped into the crowd.

Goro looked up at the small patch of sky above the alley and sighed. This was all completely unexpected, but now that he thought about it, it was not all that strange. He had never seen or met the woman who had died in Chiba, but officially, on paper, she was his wife.

"Just my luck."

At this point, the only thing he could think to do was to go see Satake, the guy who had backed him into this corner last summer. So he headed for Satake's office.

Satake Associates was a branch of a much larger organization. Among the 150 or so "organization" offices in the neighborhood, it was a latecomer.

The map of Kabuki-cho showed no clear boundaries for these criminal organizations, and their interests were all intertwined. Through all of this, a strange equilibrium ruled, and there was little room for intrusion by newcomers. But somehow or other, Satake had hung out a shingle some time after the 1980s economic bubble burst, and with ten or so young members his gang had carved out a niche, mainly by brokering day laborers.

The business was known as "promoting" day laborers, which meant of course foreigners who had come to Japan looking for menial work. For the past several years, Goro had maintained a close affiliation with Satake. Now that he was free again, it would be in his best interest to drop by, say hi, and see if there wouldn't be some new job for him to do.

Satake Associates was in an older condominium building on the far side of Shokuan-dori. It was a three-story building with only about nine apartments, but at least three of them were yakuza offices, and most of the others were probably the kinds of places where foreign women were forced to stay.

When Goro had first moved to Tokyo, mostly hostesses and bartenders lived in this area, and it was cheerful enough. Now it was always gloomy, like the rainy season only all year, as if the wind never blew and the sun never shone, and he could not believe that was just because he himself was getting long in the tooth.

Inside the building he walked down the corridor. Trays and dishes from delivery meals were stacked in front of every door. He pressed the office intercom button and smiled at the security camera over the door.

"It's Goro. Nice to see you."

The door was unlocked and opened by a young man who had often brought deliveries to Goro.

"Good to see you too. Please come on in."

The young man had the carefully shaved face—right down to the eyebrows—often seen on someone who was not long out of a motorcycle gang. It was the young members of this gang—known as "nephews"—who would bring a meal or a change of clothes when such was needed, and the cops never bothered to hassle them.

The office was a typical old-fashioned apartment, with two rooms of six tatami mats each. The front room had a bunk bed for the young gang members, while the back room was the office itself. Even this arrangement showed that Satake kept an unusually close eye on his underlings.

"Boss, Goro's here."

Seated at a steel desk, typing on a word processor, Satake looked more like a banker than a gangster as he lifted his face to look at Goro.

"Hey, how've you been? Have a seat. Satoshi, bring some coffee! Goro likes his coffee American style—weak!"

Watching the young man as he sprang to the kitchen, Goro said, "I just heard from the detective…"

"Yeah, we had a call too. You mean about Chikura, right?"

"Chikura? Oh, yeah, you mean Chikura in Chiba."

From his jacket pocket Goro produced the paper the detective had given him. He knew where Chiba was of course, but he had no idea where Chikura was.

"What am I supposed to do? The cops in Chiba asked for me by name."

"I'm not sure what you mean, Goro. There's not really much wiggle room in the matter. I have nothing to do with this. It's not my place to go."

"But you got a call too."

"Only to see if you were on your way there. It's your wife who died. It took me a minute to figure it out, but then I knew who they were talking about."

The young man brought the instant coffee.

"American, right, Satoshi?"

"Yeah."

"I want you to go with Goro. It's a lonely trip for him to make on his own. Act like a real nephew."

"Hang on just a sec," Goro said, leaning forward. "This is not as simple as you seem to think. I don't even know what this woman looked like. What if the cops or the hospital ask any questions? I wouldn't know what to say."

"I get it. Don't think so hard," Satake said soothingly. He took a binder from the desk and leafed through the thick sheaf of pages. "This is your lucky day. You're getting five hundred thousand yen for registering the marriage, and you hardly had to do a thing to earn it. They say widowers are much more attractive than divorcés. And if you don't have any other plans, I can arrange another marriage for you right away. That would be another five hundred thousand. What do you think?"

"Well, I don't like the way you're saying I'm getting this for free."

"Here we are, here we are. Hakuran Ko. You know the Chinese pronunciation? Pai-lan Kan. Nice name. Like 'Namu Amida Butsu.'"

"Pai-lan Kan, eh?"

"That's right. Well, that would be her maiden name. Changed to Pai-lan Takano when she got married. Seems her husband ran a video shop in Shinjuku. Not easy, is it, both spouses having to work? At any rate, your wife's bio is right here. Just look it over. And here's her picture and family register documents, residency card, a copy of her passport, everything's here. Oh, what's this?"

A pale blue envelope fell from between the papers. In excellent handwriting it said, "Mr. Goro Takano."

"Huh, I almost forgot about this. It arrived the day you went to jail. Could be a love letter, or maybe a will. Whatever, I'll just put it in with all the rest of this."

On top of the square envelope, Satake laid a million yen's worth of bills, still bundled in the wrappers. He put a serious look on his face.

"The first five hundred thousand is for all that you did until this morning. The second five hundred thousand is for the hospital and the crematorium and stuff like that. It might not be enough, but that's all you're getting. Got it, Goro?"

Goro and Satoshi got up, and Satake never cracked a smile.

·2·

To Goro Takano,

Yesterday morning I had a sudden stomachache, and the ambulance took me to a hospital. My customer had already left, so it was okay. I asked the hotel people, and the ambulance came.

It seems really bad, so I made up my mind to write letters to my home in China and to you, Goro. I am writing secretly, at night. The pain is so bad I can't sleep, so I am writing. I think tomorrow I will not be able to write at all. That is why I am writing secretly at night.

Thank you for marrying me. Xie-xie.

The immigration police visited me in October and again in December. But I never had to go down to the immigration office, or to the police station, because I was married to you. I was able to work the whole time.

Everyone here is kind. The organization members, the customers, everyone is kind. The ocean and the mountains are beautiful and peaceful. I would like to work here forever.

Xie-xie. That is all. I can hear the sound of the ocean. Can you hear it too?

Everyone is kind, but you Goro are the most kind. Because you married me. Xie-xie. Many thanks. Good night.

Pai-lan

"Did you know this woman?" Goro asked Satoshi as the express train left the underground platform in Tokyo Station.

"Sure, I knew her. I'm the one who took her to Chikura. Hakuran and two others. The other two, their visas ran out, so last year they were deported."

Goro looked at the sheet with Hakuran's bio. Born in 1971. Goro always had trouble understanding Western years.

"1971, how old would that make her?"

"Well, I was born in 1978, so she would have to be twenty-four or twenty-five, something like that."

"This letter has a lot of strange characters. I don't understand it all. The bio says she went to Japanese school in Shanghai or something. She spoke Japanese?"

"Yeah, she spoke Japanese really well. She spoke so well, I don't know why she had to go to Chiba. Could've worked right in Shinjuku. I think she wasn't well."

"Sick all the time?"

"Most of them are sick most of the time. Doesn't have to be AIDS or anything like that, but it's hard on the liver. Viral hepatitis. And they never go to a doctor, so they end up with cirrhosis. They're young and all, but they're dead before you know it. You know, they all think they can make these strange teas and Chinese herbal medicine and just drink that and they'll get better."

"You seem to know a lot about this."

"It's my business."

Satoshi wore a necktie that seemed unsuited to his baby face, and he loosened it. Almost proudly, he started to talk about the difficulties of his work. For managers in his line of work, women were the product, so minding their health was crucial.

"It's important to go to the doctor early, even if it seems like nothing, but they're afraid their illegal status will be discovered, so they don't want to go. They don't have insurance cards, so they worry about what it will cost to go to the doctor, and they get all bloated, and then the customers lose interest in them. By the time the ambulance comes for them it's usually too late."

"Is that so."

Satoshi tried to get a peek at the letter.

"Wow, incredible handwriting. The sentences are hard to understand, though."

"What did you expect? The Chinese use *kanji* for everything."

"Sad, isn't it? All that 'thanks for marrying me' stuff."

"I don't know if what I did was a good thing or a bad thing. What do you think?"

"Well, she's thanking you, so it must have been a good thing."

The train emerged into waning daylight. Along the coast, the lights were coming on in the tall buildings. A spring rain pelted the train windows in diagonal streaks.

"We don't have any umbrellas with us, do we?"

"I told you we should have waited 'til tomorrow morning to make this trip."

"Are you crazy? Your wife dies and you want to wait a day?"

"Wasn't there somebody with a driver's license?"

"Sorry, but everybody else had other things to do. They're running around all over Japan."

"I should've just asked the boss."

"No good, no good. If the police in Chiba figured out that connection it would be all over."

When the snacks trolley came down the aisle, Goro bought a beer.

"I don't drink. I'll have an oolong tea. Goro, don't drink too much, okay? Remember, your wife just died, and we're going to get her body, so you can't show up drunk, okay?"

"You think I could get through this without a drink? Think about it, I just got out of the clink this morning. I really should be celebrating my release."

Goro felt the cold beer slide down his parched throat. It tasted bitter. It tasted strange.

"I just don't get it. I don't understand what's going on at all. What have I done here? Never saw her face. Just learned her name today. I can understand marrying someone you don't know. What I can't understand is not getting to know the woman you marry. And the first time you meet her it's her dead body. It's like a story in some manga, you know what I mean? *Manga!*"

Goro mumbled to himself as he ruffled through the papers and took out her picture, and then he shut his mouth.

"Satoshi, is this her? Holy crap!"

It was a small passport photo.

"Yeah, she was hot. When I took her out to Chiba, I was getting all excited just sitting next to her. Actually, this photo doesn't do her justice. I thought I'd have to go out there again sometime just to have a little fun, on the sly, know what I'm saying?"

That beautiful name, Pai-lan Kan, came back to Goro's ears like music.

"What did that Satake think he was trying to pull over on me? Somebody like this, I would've married her for real."

"No way, Goro. This is business. You'd have to pay off the whole debt and pay a penalty on top of that. That would be a pile of money. Just the advance would be three million, and then you have to think of future earnings and handling fees—that would be at least double. The boss doesn't lie about stuff like that."

"So, Satake has lost a pile of money."

"I wouldn't say lost, exactly, but let's say this has upset his plans. When that phone call came he got really pissed off, and all the other guys got out of there fast. But then he just handed over a million to you, and I guess that says a lot. It made me appreciate him all over again."

The rain came down harder than ever.

·3·

Most of the passengers got out at Kisarazu. The train ran alongside the deep black of the ocean, and the gleaming lights of the petrochemical plants faded into the distance.

The last of the other passengers got off in Tateyama, and at Chikura, the last stop, Goro and Satoshi were the only ones on the platform. A misty spring rain swirled around the searchlight like smoke.

In the waiting room there was not a soul, just a gray cat sleeping on a bench. The clock said eight, but Goro had his doubts.

There was just one taxi. The driver leaned against the wheel and sized up his prospective passengers. Satoshi emerged from the phone booth.

"He said we should go to the office first. There's a right way to do these things."

"I don't like it. If anybody asks me anything, I don't know a thing."

"Don't worry. I'm just going to pay my respects. You can wait in the car."

"You think you're going to be able to take care of this business?"

Satoshi didn't like the sound of that, and he raised one carefully shaved eyebrow.

"The two bosses have already settled this, so I'm just going to say hello. We're here already."

Goro thought this was way too easy. From the rainy end of the train platform he had seen the neon lights of several drinking establishments, hazy in the mist. He could smell saltwater.

This must have been some sort of bad dream. If he woke up back in the common room at the jail, the story of this dream would be a hit among the other prisoners.

But if this was real life...Goro tried to put himself in the place of the woman, his unseen wife, who had arrived at this train station last summer. For that woman, this end of the line must have been a forsaken place. She must have thought she had fallen as low as she could possibly fall, into hell itself.

"Should be simple," Goro agreed and got into the taxi.

They had not gone far before the few buildings clustered

near the station gave way to farm fields and woods on both sides of the road. They descended a gentle slope toward the ocean. In the darkness, headlights passed like shooting stars along the coastal highway. On the far side of the pine forest must have been the ocean.

"Nice place, don't you think, Goro?" Satoshi wiped the window with the elbow of his out-of-character double-breasted suit.

"Who could tell if it's nice or not nice in the dark?"

"No resort hotels, no condominiums. Just summer houses and a few company properties. The beach is always empty. Last summer I came here and swam with them."

"Who do you mean, 'them'?"

"The girls. I bought them bathing suits, and we swam on that beach. I think Hakuran had a blue bikini."

"Thanks for doing that," Goro said without thinking. Something was wrong. He could think of nothing but the wife he had never met, and that put him in a black mood. Satoshi kept talking because he thought Goro must be kidding.

"Filipinas are all tiny, but Chinese girls are tall, with long legs, just like fashion models. And their skin is beautiful. It was the first time they ever swam in the ocean, and all three of them had a great time.

Goro imagined a vivid scene, Hakuran gamboling in the surf. The image of her, dancing in the summer sun in a blue bikini, was dazzling.

Finally the car stopped in front of a building that faced the shore. It was a two-story white house, covered in a heavy coat of white paint. There were jutting windows with little blinking lights and a sign with a suitable name. The rain fell like smoke, and the neon lights buzzed angrily.

Satoshi left the car waiting and climbed the iron staircase at the side of the building. On the first floor there was a bar, and on the second floor was an office. In a window facing the sea hung some forgotten underwear, wet with rain.

"Place like this, customers come here?"

The driver removed his hat and, yawning, answered, "You bet. After the last train, if I just hang around here in the car, I get plenty of customers all the way to the motel."

"Guys from around here?"

"Naw, guys from around here don't come here much. Afraid who might see 'em. Mostly guys who come here fishing, or guys who come to a company beach house."

Now Goro thought that wasn't a bad idea at all, a little bit of fishing, a nice girl while you're here. Come up the night before, take a girl to a motel, get an early boat the next morning. Now that would be an efficient approach to things. Spend some time at the company beach house with some like-minded individuals, that would be lots more fun than a trip to some boring old hot springs.

"I suppose there are places like this all over Japan. Cops aren't as much trouble as in some hot spot like Tokyo. And out here there isn't much else fun to do, so they don't even try to catch you, 'cause if they do..."

Barely five minutes had gone by before Satoshi came back down the stairs. He hadn't lied about keeping the conversation simple.

"They asked if we were going to take away her personal effects, but there's nothing you want, right, Goro? There aren't any valuables, and nothing in the savings account. Don't really know, of course."

Goro was skeptical that the woman would have been penniless, but he was in no position to complain. All he knew was that for eight months, since last summer, she had lived here.

The car headed away from the shore. Goro gazed out the rear window. The white house in the pine glade seemed like an apparition.

The car stopped in front of a tiny police station, and Goro readied himself. He wrote the woman's name with his fingertip and rattled off her birthday.

Just twelve hours before he had been released from police custody in Shinjuku.

"I'm going to have to show ID. I hate this. Today of all days."

"Don't worry so much. It's not as if you killed her. Do you have some kind of identification?"

Goro didn't have a driver's license or a passport. He had no credit cards. He found an insurance ID card in the inside pocket of his jacket. Not because he expected to use it if he ever got sick or injured. He had it so he could borrow money from the neighborhood moneylenders.

"Insurance ID okay, you think?"

"Sure, that'll be fine. Maybe it even has your wife's name on it."

It was a brand-new card from the National Health office. Now that Satoshi mentioned it, Goro noticed for the first time that "Hakuran Takano" was listed as a beneficiary.

"I forgot all about that. Shucks, that's convenient. We might have to pay the hospital or something."

It was the police station of a peaceful harbor town. The policewoman at the reception desk had a bright smile, like a young woman working in some bank.

When she heard why they were there, though, her facial expression changed to show her condolence. A middle-aged police captain emerged carrying some paperwork. The name on his chest badge was not the name Goro had been given in Shinjuku. Maybe that guy had been on the early shift.

"So, you're the husband?"

"That's right. Takano. I'm sorry for all your trouble."

The police captain looked at Goro with suspicion, then cast his eyes on Satoshi's sharp suit.

"And this is…?"

"My son."

Goro thought that would sound better than "nephew,"

and he said it as soon as it popped into his head. The difference in their ages was about right.

"Your son? But not the son of the deceased..."

"That's right. He's the son of my previous wife. But Hakuran always loved him."

Under the counter, Satoshi stepped on Goro's toes, as if to say, *Don't say anything more than you have to.*

"Do you have some form of identification?"

"Will my insurance ID do?"

The policeman noted down Goro's insurance ID number and his address.

"I notice your son isn't listed here."

"Yes, he's officially registered as part of my previous wife's family. But her new husband's no good, so things aren't going so well. That's part of the reason why he always got along better with my new wife than with his own mother."

Satoshi stepped harder on Goro's foot. Goro didn't care if he told a lie, he just wanted to make the connection between himself and Hakuran seem like they had really been a couple.

"I finally got things cleared up with my wife, and nothing seemed to be in the way of us living together again. We had been separated for some time, and I didn't even know she was sick. She didn't want to cause any trouble. That's the kind of woman she was."

Satoshi started to pull away, but Goro reached out and pulled his hand to him. Satoshi was trembling with fear.

"Well, I'm sure you got a lot going on in your life. I'm sorry for your loss. Let me tell you how to get to the hospital."

Satoshi relaxed. It seemed the police officer was not going to probe any further. He spread out a map and gave them directions to the hospital.

"They'll take care of everything else for you there. Thanks for your trouble."

It was all too simple, Goro thought to himself.

All the faces of the past ten days—the detectives who had interrogated him about this and that, all the grouchy guards—came before him one by one. The wife he had never known, who had been hounded all her life, investigated to death—now she was dead, and it was all over with the words, "Thanks for your trouble."

"Is that it? The police don't need to know anything else?"

The police officer had already stood up and started to leave, but turned back as Goro asked, "You don't require any explanation? For your reports, your paperwork?"

"No, that won't be necessary."

"Why not?"

Goro was getting agitated, and Satoshi tugged at his sleeve.

"What do you mean, why not? It wasn't a suspicious death. The police normally only get involved when a person is already dead when the body is discovered, or if someone passes away within twenty-four hours of being hospitalized. In other words, when it isn't clear what happened. Then a medical examiner performs an investigation, and sometimes an autopsy is mandated. In your wife's case, the circumstances were clear."

Goro started to answer back, but Satoshi forcibly pulled him away from the desk.

"I'm sorry, my father is a little upset. This was all so sudden. Dad, let's go."

Goro bit back whatever it was he had to say: *I sold a place in my family register for five hundred thousand yen. I never even saw that woman. She came from someplace in the countryside in China, had never even seen the ocean before, was forced to be a plaything for the yakuza, fell deep into debt, and died before she could see a doctor. You don't find that "suspicious"? You think the "circumstances were clear"? What the hell. I think it's plenty strange.*

"Goro. Knock it off. What's the matter with you?" Satoshi said under his breath as they headed straight for the exit.

"This is all too simple. I don't understand what Satake is up to, I don't understand what the local boss here is up to, and I don't understand what you're up to either. A person is dead."

"Just shut up, Goro. Get a grip."

"What did that policeman mean, the 'circumstances were clear'? I don't think anything is clear here. Why would a woman from China come to some foreign country, to this bleak country town, in the first place? And then some guy claiming to be her husband pops up to claim the body. Something is wrong here. There is absolutely nothing clear about these circumstances."

"Actually, it's very clear," Satoshi said as he stuffed Goro into the taxi.

"What are you talking about? What is clear? Why don't those idiot cops see what's strange about this? She's dead, so nobody has any use for her anymore."

"You've got it all wrong. They know everything, can't you see that? Think about this for a minute, Goro. They called the jail in Tokyo, and they called our office. They know everything. Everything is clear."

"So why didn't they take me in? Why didn't they arrest Satake? Or you?"

"How should I know? The law has nothing to say about this."

"Don't joke around. Solicitation of prostitution. Illegal employment. Abduction and confinement. I got ten days for selling porn videos to old lechers, but how come everybody's okay about this? We all killed that woman."

Satoshi clucked his tongue and gave Goro a shove.

"Give me a break, Goro. Don't be an idiot. Ten days in the slammer and you went completely ga-ga?"

The car drove down the highway along the shore, heading for the hospital.

·4·

It was a magnificent hospital, totally out of place in the little harbor town.

According to the taxi driver, the local notables were intent on replicating completely American-style health care, and they had brought in all the best doctors and installed the most advanced medical equipment. He said patients came from the big university hospitals in Tokyo, and even from foreign countries.

The on-call doctor's explanation was simple: cirrhosis of the liver, causing fluid to accumulate in the abdomen. This was eliminated, and the patient's condition stabilized for a while, but on the third day a vein burst and there was nothing more they could do to save her. For as long as she maintained consciousness, the patient continued to deny the hospital permission to contact her family, in other words Goro.

An older nurse showed them the way to the underground mortuary. The room was surprisingly bright and sparkling clean. The two men sat in steel chairs and waited awhile until the nurse returned, wheeling the gurney down the hallway toward them.

"Don't worry. She looks beautiful. Here we embalm, just like in America."

The nurse positioned the gurney in the middle of the white room, pulled back the vinyl sheet, and there was a woman's face, too pretty to be dead.

"We remove the blood and replace it with embalming fluid. She's been in the refrigerator, so the body is cold, but her facial color is good, don't you think?"

She was indeed a beautiful woman. As the thought crossed his mind that this had been his wife, Goro put his palms to his chilled cheeks and let out a loud sob.

The nurse pressed her hands together in a prayerful gesture and left, and Satoshi nervously shook Goro's shoulders.

"Goro, get a grip on yourself. What's the matter with you?"

Goro himself thought something must be wrong with him. He couldn't remember having ever cried in his life, even as a child.

"It's sad, I know. Nothing to be crying about though. Goro, you're making a scene. Knock it off."

Why did he feel so sad about the death of this foreign woman, someone he didn't even know? He felt as if he were standing beside himself, looking skeptically on as his eyes welled with unceasing tears, and he wept, howling like an animal.

"We still have a lot to get done. Tomorrow we have to go to the town office and take care of the paperwork. Have to have the cremation and take the bones back to Tokyo. We have to call the crematorium. I'll make the call, if you don't mind."

Satoshi sighed as he left the room, just as the nurse came back with a cot and a blanket.

"Feel free to use these if you like. Maybe you need some rest."

Slowly, Goro came to himself, came to realize the source of his sadness. He had felt strange ever since reading the woman's letter, when he was still on the train.

He knelt beside the gurney and rested his face on the woman's abdomen. Rain pattered against the window of the underground chamber, and he could hear the surf roaring nearby.

The words of her letter came back to him.

Everyone here is kind. The organization members, the customers, everyone is kind. The ocean and the mountains are beautiful and peaceful. I would like to work here forever.

Xie-xie. That is all. I can hear the sound of the ocean. Can you hear it too?

Goro considered that he had lived twenty years in a town without a trace of kindness.

That night, he had a dream.

He was back in his hometown in the north, which he had left long ago.

When the tide goes out in the Sea of Okhotsk, sandbars are exposed where the fisher folk find a wealth of clams and oysters.

The Sea of Okhotsk never froze, and the tide always ebbed and flowed, even when the ice floes came floating down the ocean currents from beyond. There was nothing fun to do in the fishing village, but the people never starved.

His older brother, rowing toward the cliffs, said, "Goro, your bride sure is beautiful! Twenty years in Tokyo you finally found a fish worth reeling in!"

"Shut up, you're embarrassing me! Hey, hey!"

Hakuran stood in front of the watch hut, waving. Two children were playing at her feet.

"Beautiful, kind, too good for you."

"Brother, I think I want to live here forever. What do you think of that?"

"You won't hear any complaints from me. There's more than enough clams and oysters here for all of us. You, your wife, your two kids, hardly a drop in the bucket."

"You think Mom and Dad will be okay with that? I didn't come home for their funerals."

"I don't see any problem. The only regret they ever had was that you weren't here. It'll make them happy."

The little boat came to a halt, its bow now pointed toward shore, where a fog was rising.

"Say, where have they gone? Pai-lan! Pai-lan!"

Goro wandered the beach, searching for his wife and children. Looking behind him, he saw that the white fog had swallowed the sea.

"Goro..."

He could hear Pai-lan's voice, like a bell tinkling. The dry sand sucked at his boots up to the ankles, and he felt hobbled.

He held his hand to his mouth and called to his wife, "Where are you?"

"Goro..." came the reply. Following the sound of her voice, he climbed a dune.

"Goro, I am dead. I cannot live with you any longer."

"That can't be! I've come back to be with you. Why would you say such a thing? I will do anything for you, I will do whatever I can to make you happy. All the pain of your past, I will make it up to you. You can't die. We're going to the hospital. I'll carry you on my back. Come with me to the hospital. They'll take care of your liver there."

In the fog, Goro leaned over and thrust out his backside.

"Never mind, Goro. It's all right. Thank you. *Xie-xie*."

At his feet bloomed shocking pink rugosa roses.

"Why is this happening to you? We can't not live together. You won't be able to eat, you won't be able to drink, you won't be able to sleep with me."

The flowers trembled as if they were whispering.

"Thank you, Goro. I've had enough. My customers have all been kind, but you have been the most kind. Because you married me."

Goro's tears dripped on the flowers.

"Kind? What have I ever done that was kind? All the yakuza, all the cops, all the customers, did nothing but hassle you. And I was the worst of all. I sold a place in my family register for five hundred thousand yen, and I spent all the money in three days. And you had to pay that money back with your body. Spitting up blood the whole time, you had to pay it back. All of us are demons, demons who ate you up, down to the bones. There's nothing kind about demons."

Embracing the wordless rose bush whole, Goro raised his

voice, putting all of his emotions into it. "You'll never have to do another thing. Just marry me, please."

·5·

The gray sea, pelted by the rain, rushed past the windows of the express train.

The bones in his lap stayed warm the whole trip.

"Come on, Goro, just give me a little of the money. You made me do everything," Satoshi said as he sank into his seat, yawning, exhausted.

"You must have learned a lot this trip. And now you're going to be the chief fixer in Kabuki-cho. Stuff like this is going to happen to you all the time."

"Quit kidding around. You're the one who got the money, and all you did was cry the whole time. All I'm getting here is my regular pay, and I had to be nice to the monk. Who's the idiot? You want a beer?"

Satoshi bought some drinks and snacks from the cart that came rolling down the aisle. He chugged the unfamiliar beer.

"They could take you in for that."

"Leave me be. I'd rather be in juvie than this. But Goro, tell me the truth. You didn't know a thing about that woman?"

"I swear. I didn't know anything."

"I can't believe it. Listen, I won't tell the boss, but just tell me the truth. How many times did you do her?"

Goro turned away, looking out at the twilight sea.

"Goro, you should go to the hospital yourself, get checked out. You heard what the doctor said last night: 'Viral hepatitis rarely shows symptoms.' He told you. Wouldn't be good if you got it."

"No reason I should have it. I never even met her."

"That can't be. That has to be a lie. What was all that crying about, just for show? You were lying right on the corpse, bawling. At the crematorium, in front of the oven, I thought you were going to collapse. You were gasping as we collected the bones. It was embarrassing."

"If I was that good at acting, I could have been somebody. I was crying because I felt so sorry for her. I couldn't help it."

"That's pretty hard to believe."

"If you stick around Kabuki-cho another twenty years it'll come to you. Or haven't you got the guts for it?"

Goro recalled the lonely funeral.

In a small room at the crematorium, the monk stood and chanted a simple sutra. It was a simple farewell ceremony, attended by only a few foreign women in their everyday clothes. Even those women appeared to be there only because they'd been ordered to. None of them were crying.

In Goro's hand, he could still feel how light the bones were as he picked them up with the special chopsticks. The women behaved badly, making no move to participate in the bone-picking. Goro did it all himself, placing the bones in the urn, leaving not even the smallest.

It had been just one day since he had received his instructions from Satake, and now everything was taken care of. It had not been at all difficult. Leave out the useless prayers and customs, and a human death was not that complicated.

From Satoshi's point of view, the one thing he could have done without was Goro's unbelievable sadness. And Goro could understand why Satoshi was angry.

"Goro, have a drink. You must be thirsty from all your crying."

Satoshi was angry, but Goro could see he was starting to understand him better. The boy was smart and quick-witted. He wouldn't have a half-assed life like Goro's.

The beer flowed down his gullet, which was tired and parched from crying. The chill of it spread through his empty stomach, making the bones in his lap feel all the warmer.

The can still to his mouth, Satoshi said, "Ah," as if he had just remembered something. "I wonder what the boss is going to do with the bones. Send them back to China?"

He'd never go to that much trouble, Goro thought to himself. No matter what was going to happen, send them home, find some no-name cemetery, it was Goro who was going to have to take care of it.

"It's all part of the 'consideration' I got, that too. What do you think?"

"Gimme a break, Goro. I have no clue."

What was happening? Outside the window, the fishing villages had disappeared, and huge industrial complexes stood like castles, spewing orange flames into the dark night.

"So, shall we have a look at what we've got here? Maybe there's some money."

They had received a paper bag from the hospital, and now Satoshi retrieved it from the overhead shelf. They had brought it this far without looking inside.

"Takano" was written on it. Maybe the nurse had written it.

Satoshi removed the tape and pulled the contents from the bag, one object at a time. A thin coat, a dress made of some synthetic material, a pair of small silver sandals.

"We should've just put this stuff straight into the coffin. What're we going to do with it now? Just give it to some bitch."

"No you won't. It's not yours."

Goro grabbed the bag. A small red purse rolled out.

"A bag! It's got money in it, I'll bet. They like to carry cash. We'll split it, right Goro?"

The purse held a small amount of money and some condoms. And a flaming red lipstick.

"Three thousand yen and some change. Not worth fussing over."

"You can have it."

"Really? Thanks!"

Next came a folded envelope. It was a letter, the same blue as the earlier one. "To Goro Takano," it said in beautiful handwriting. Seeing it, Goro felt heat in his chest.

"Look, another love letter. 'Goro is the kindest...' and all that crap."

Goro smashed Satoshi's nose with the heel of his palm.

"Hey, that hurts! What do you think you're doing?"

"Shut up! Get out of here!"

"I'm sorry," Satoshi said, slinking to another seat on the other side of the aisle.

Goro unfolded the letter. Unlike yesterday's letter, this time the pale blue paper was covered with dense, jumbled writing.

My dearest Goro,

I am writing this letter in secret while no one else is here. I'm writing lying down with one hand, and I'm sorry the letters look awful.

I haven't talked to anybody since I arrived at the hospital. If I speak Japanese, people will ask me all kinds of things, so I've only spoken Chinese.

I know I'm going to die. The doctors have been talking about it, thinking that I don't understand Japanese. I also know because I know a lot of other girls like me. My time has come.

The kind nurse is writing as much as she can and asked for my family's phone number. I told her Satake's number. I'm sorry. I figured the police know everything anyway.

Goro, I think I know everything about you. Satake wrote me a lot about you—your address, your age, your personality, your habits, the foods you like—in case I got arrested, and I remember all of it. I read his note every day so I wouldn't forget.

I have a picture of you too. Four copies of the same one. I

always have them with me. I look at them every day so I won't forget, and I have really learned to like you. And because I like you, my work is hard for me. Before I work, I always apologize to you. There's nothing I can do about it, but I'm sorry.

So I work hard, and I pay back the money I owe, and when that's done I wanted to meet you. I thought I could live with you. That's what I thought as I worked as hard as I could. But I can't anymore.

Goro, you're always smiling. You don't smoke you only drink a little you never fight you don't like meat you like fish. So I quit smoking too. I drink only a little I don't eat meat I eat fish.

My customers are all kind, but I never forget you, even when I'm working. It's the truth. I think of my customers as you. And when I do, I do my best, and my customers are happy.

You were born in a place by the sea, weren't you? When I came here, I thought it must be nearby, and I looked on a map. It made me sad when I realized how very far it is. But it's the same for me. You traveled far to do your work, and so did I.

If I die, will you come to see me?

If I am able to meet you, I have just one favor to ask.

Please bury me in your grave. May I die as your wife? Please forgive me for asking such a thing. But this is the only thing I will ever ask of you.

Thanks to you, I was able to work a lot, and I was able to send a lot of money home. I am afraid of dying, and it hurts, and it is painful, but I can bear it. Just hear my plea, please.

I can hear the sound of the sea. It is raining. It is very dark. I'm writing lying down, with one hand, and I'm sorry the letters look awful.

Goro, I love you. The most in the world. More than anyone else, I love you. Not because it hurts or because I'm in pain or because I'm afraid, but I'm crying as I think of you. Every night when I go to sleep I look at your photograph and I cry and say good night to you. It's always the same, I look at your kind photograph and the tears come. Not because I am sad or hurting, my tears come because I am thanking you.

There is nothing I have to give to you, and I am sorry. Only words and scrawled letters. I am sorry.

I love you from the bottom of my heart more than anyone else in the world.

Goro-san Goro-san Goro-san Goro-san Goro-san Goro-san Goro-san Goro-san Goro-san.

Tsai-chien. Sayonara.

From about the middle of the letter, Goro was crying, audibly.

"What's the matter, Goro?"

Goro turned to Satoshi, who wore a timid expression, and threw the empty can at him.

"Shut up! Get out of here!"

"But Goro, this isn't normal…"

"It is too normal. What's it to you anyway? You're all the ones who aren't normal. Not a single one of you, not normal at all."

Outside the window, the lights of the industrial plant swept closer through the dark night.

Goro would go home. His older brother would welcome him warmly. He would be happy to meet his younger brother's wife, whom he had never met.

"Pai-lan. Let's go home. They're all waiting for us."

Goro took the old lipstick and on the box of bones wrote, "Pai-lan Takano."

"I can't write as nicely as you, but don't tease me about it."

As he cried and laughed at the same time, the dry bones in his lap rattled.

Devil

I have seen the Devil.

Whether you believe me or not, I am certain of the day I first saw the Devil, with his two curved horns and his giant wings and his whole body covered with wet black fur.

The house I was born in stood out, even among the affluent villas of the Yamanote district. If children were in the next yard playing baseball, for example, and hit their precious ball over the wall into my yard, they would not be able to come ask for it, or even to sneak in and get it themselves. I, who had no friends in the neighborhood, would hear their cheers and grab my glove and go out into the garden and wait forever for a ball to come over the wall. What I really wanted was to play baseball with them, but that was strictly forbidden. All I could do was to play the extra, unseen outfielder, throwing back the foul balls.

I lived in that house until I was in the middle of fifth grade. Why is it that my memories always seem bathed in red, like a sunset landscape? I think it may be because the house was in the middle of a grove of sumac and cherry trees, luxuriously intertwined. At certain times of the year the whole place—the ponds, the lawns, the man-made hills, the old samurai main house, and the separate Western wing—all seemed to be bathed in red.

It was during one such season that I first saw the man in question come strolling up the pebble path to the gabled entrance, just at the moment of dusk.

I had snuck into the maid's room beside the front entrance, and I was secretly watching television. It was a time when people would crowd around outdoor TVs in front of train stations, but in our house we had a foreign-made television set even in the maid's room. My TV viewing time was strictly limited, so I would often steal off to the maid's room to sneak a few extra minutes.

"Pardon me, is anyone at home?"

The tatami-floored entryway was just like a Zen temple, complete with a wooden mallet and thwacking board, but the man could only stand there calling out repeatedly for someone.

My mother went to the door. The servants always made the corridor floors squeak as they trotted around, but my mother walked deliberately, as if she were polishing the floor with the soles of her *tabi* socks. I could tell it was my mother by the sound of her gait.

I hurriedly shut off the TV, slid open the cedar door, and peered at the main entrance. I could not see my mother as she knelt by the partition screen.

"My name is Kageyama. The student department of Tokyo University sent me," the man said, standing just outside the dimly lit main entryway. Over his student uniform he wore a manteau, old-fashioned even for that time. His face, in the shadow cast by the brim of his peaked hat in the frosty lamplight, could not be seen. In the dusky gloom it was as if a ball of blackness had suddenly emerged from nowhere.

My mother's white hand extended from her place beside the screen. The man entered without removing his hat, and he sat down on the step where my mother indicated.

My mother took her time reading the letter of introduction he presented. It was not the sort of thing that should have deserved such scrutiny, but that was my mother's way: she took everything slowly.

That's when the man noticed me peering at him through the crack in the cedar door. Actually, "noticed" isn't quite the right word. He looked me straight in the face, as if he had known all along that I was there hiding in the maid's room. And then he smiled a crooked smile, using just half of his thin lips.

The lantern on the earthen floor cast some light on the man's face, but his thick eyeglasses reflected the light back a bright white, so his expression was indiscernible.

"It says here you're in the medical department," said my mother from the shadows of the partition screen.

"That's right. Third year."

"And you're from, what is this, Hoten? Repatriated from Manchuria, I see. A military family?"

"No. My father worked for the railway in Manchuria. He died while we were over there. Will that be an issue?"

My mother thought for a while before responding. "Not at all. Our forebears were samurai, so I would prefer not to have someone with a strong dialect or a countrified way of speaking. But if you're from Manchuria, I don't suppose that will be a problem."

After that, my mother and the man continued talking, but with awkward silences.

I learned a few things about the man: he was studying medicine at Tokyo University, and he had a rented room in Yanaka. His father was dead, and he was getting a scholarship, but money was still short. This would be his second experience with tutoring. The pupil he had tutored last year had entered Azabu Middle School in the spring.

"So weekdays from five to nine will be all right? We will provide an evening meal."

"That would be a great help. I am just a poor student. By the way..."

At that point, the man turned the conversation rather clumsily into a negotiation about pay. He said the terms offered by the student office were lower than last year, and he wondered if my mother wouldn't be willing to reconsider them. The man said he was an honor student in the department of medicine and had experience as a tutor. He was coming on a bit strong.

My mother, who was unaccustomed to negotiating, gave in.

"About your meals, are there any foods you don't care for?"

"Not especially. Not at all. I eat anything."

As the man got up, he glanced my way again and gave me an eerie smile.

"Ah, there is just one more thing…" my mother started to say, as if she had just remembered, grabbing the cuff of his manteau with her white hand. "Do you have any special beliefs?"

"You mean religion? I am an atheist."

"That will be quite all right. My son is attending a mission school. But none of us are Christian. Still, we find the differences among the various sects, well, you know…"

The man fixed me in his gaze. The smile was gone from his lips.

"Don't you worry, ma'am. I believe in neither God nor Buddha."

"I'm happy to hear that."

The man started to head for the main gate, but while still within the circle of the lamplight he bowed politely. Then he sped quickly down the pebble path, which was by now the color of sumac trees burning.

At elementary school I had a close friend named Hashiguchi, the son of a noble family. He had asthma and was often absent from school, so he had a tutor at home. This made him a good student, but I was tired of hearing about his strict but slightly creepy tutor.

Inwardly, I felt sorry for him. This went above and beyond the tutor. Because of his strict schedule, Hashiguchi never had any time to watch TV, and he was always left out of the next day's conversations about it at school.

With his portable inhaler, and straining to participate in the class discussions about television, Hashiguchi was the epitome of an unhappy child.

When I imagined the same things happening to me, my vision turned black. So on the Sunday night before my own home tutelage was to begin, I thought of a plan, and I decided to consult with my mother. I would ask her if my lessons could not be curtailed by one hour or shifted in some way, so that I would be able to keep up socially with my classmates.

My mother told me to ask my father. My father was seldom home, but that day he happened to be there. A horse he owned had won a big race, so he was at home with a large entourage. I stepped down from the main house and walked along the garden to the Western wing, where the victory celebration was taking place in the reception room facing the terrace. My father was in the game room with a few guests for a round of billiards.

A geisha with a traditional hairstyle sat by the hearth with a scoreboard that looked like a monstrous abacus, and she was keeping score in the game of four-ball and calling out the numbers in a strange voice: "Te-en, twooo."

Everyone who saw me and recognized me had some flattering comment at the ready. I, however, was unable to respond simply to these ordinary pleasantries. I knew that as the evening wore on my father and his friends would go off somewhere.

My father heard my plea, leaning across the felt table, his cue in his hands. The whole time, he was adjusting his hand position this way and that and applying fresh blue chalk to the end of the cue, and I wondered if he was even listening to me at all.

I asked him again, and he looked at me across the pool table and threw the chalk at me.

Had it not been for the servant boy standing nearby, who dropped the silver platter he was carrying so that he could physically restrain me, I might have thrown myself headfirst into the fireplace. The boy was able to save me at the last possible moment, just before I thrust myself into the blazing flames.

Instead of me, it was the boy who suffered burns when his hands landed in the glowing coals. After a bit of a ruckus, my father and his entourage and the geisha went off somewhere.

On Monday morning I arrived at school, stepped out of the Packard, and immediately had an uneasy feeling. There were no children playing in the schoolyard, and the old, ivy-covered school building just stood there, silent.

The maid helped me carry my bag, and as we entered the school, instead of the usual spritely minuet coming over the speakers, there was a dismal dirge.

Hashiguchi, who had been hospitalized for his asthma, had died the night before.

On his school desk, which was right next to mine, were flowers. We had all gone to see him in the hospital the week before, and after our visit he had seemed quite healthy and accompanied us to the main entrance. Apparently late Sunday night he had suffered a sudden attack and stopped breathing.

Instead of Monday morning assembly there was a memorial mass for Hashiguchi. After the mass, I was summoned to the staff room and asked to give a eulogy at the funeral the next day. I was both a close friend of Hashiguchi's and a class officer, so there was no way I could get out of it.

It was a completely depressing day. Instead of gym class that day we had free time, and I spent it alone in the staff room practicing my eulogy.

And after that, what would be waiting for me at home but

the start of my lessons with that creepy new tutor.

At five o'clock on the dot, Kageyama arrived.

A heavy squeaking I had never heard before came down the hallway. Looking across the inner garden, I could see him coming, led by my mother, sliding down the hallway, dressed all in black. In the late afternoon sun shining through the uneven glass panes, his long shadow stretched starkly across the paper screens of the spacious drawing room.

Kageyama entered my room, and his thick glasses shone as he cursorily examined my bookshelves, beetle specimens, and plastic model collection. Once he had removed his hat, his face seemed peculiarly long, like a horse or a goat. His student uniform gave off a mixed odor of sweat and disinfectant that made me feel nauseous.

"What a nice room you have. An ideal environment," he said in a low voice.

"We had just this room remodeled in Western style. For studying, it's best to have a desk and chair," my mother said.

Kageyama ran his knobby finger over my desk.

"Mahogany?" he asked.

"No, it's ebony. A hand-me-down from his father."

My mother, standing next to Kageyama, came up only to his chest. After she introduced me, she said, "A very close friend of my son's passed away last night, and he seems to be a bit down about it. Please go easy on him today."

If I was a little upset that day, it had less to do with Hashi-guchi's death than with the fact that I now had a cursed tutor, just as he had had.

"The boy this tutor taught last year got into Azabu Middle School. I expect no less from you if you apply yourself," my mother said as she left, leaving me feeling unbelievably depressed.

The first thing Kageyama did was to spend an awfully long time going through my notes and test papers. When he was done he pronounced, "You're really dumb, aren't you."

I felt like the first thing he had done upon meeting me was to punch me in the face. Never in my life had I ever been confronted with such rudeness, not from my parents, and not from my teachers.

My study room, which jutted from the house like a bat's claws and faced the grassy yard, received a lot of western sun. Powerful branches of the zelkova trees along the outer wall cast dark shadows like cracks on the red-dyed wall of the room.

Suddenly I remembered vividly something Hashiguchi used to say, when he was still well, first thing in the morning upon arriving at his seat in the classroom:

"I swear, that guy is the Devil himself..."

A lot of people lived in my household. In the main house, there was my mother, me, my grandfather, and several servants, and across the garden, on the second floor of the Western annex, were seven or eight people who worked for my father.

Every morning at the designated time, the men of the household gathered together in a tatami-mat room off the kitchen area, my grandfather and I in the seats of honor, to eat breakfast from lacquered boxes and trays. One step lower, in a wood-floored area, were the trays for my mother and the maids.

It was a horrible custom of the old houses of Tokyo that all the men, including the drivers and the gardeners, ate together in the big tatami room, while the women ate sitting on a wooden floor, even the mothers.

I did not know very much about my grandfather's past. There was a family business, and my father had made it grow, so my grandfather did not even have enough weight to be called head of the household.

In all likelihood, he had buried the first half of his life

together with his army officer's uniform. His natural reticence was like that of a monk or priest, and he spent a good portion of each day in front of an altar, whether Buddhist or Shinto.

It seemed strange to me that a man of such integrity would get along so badly with my mother. While they never quarreled publicly, the negative energy was palpable.

My going to a Christian school may well have been one form of my mother's rebellion against my grandfather. Instead of approving, my grandfather inculcated in me the custom of paying homage to the Shinto and Buddhist gods every morning before school.

My father was seldom at home, and my mother and my grandfather were almost always at odds. In other words, no household in the world was both as affluent and as fragile as ours. Without a doubt, this was a mouth-watering enticement for the Devil.

Kageyama arrived at exactly five o'clock every day. Without a superfluous word, he would sit down next to me and begin a demanding lesson that allowed not even an extra breath. The only break was thirty minutes for dinner at seven o'clock. Sitting side by side in silence on the sofa, Kageyama and I would eat from the trays the maids brought us.

Harder for me than the actual studying was that I had to spend four hours every day face to face with Kageyama.

Everything about this arrangement was unpleasant. From his long, unsmiling face, to his toothless manner of speaking, to his habit of chewing noisily, it was all more than I could bear.

My grades, of course, improved by leaps and bounds. On the academic aptitude tests I had to take each month, the things Kageyama told me about always seemed to appear, as if by magic. It was as if Kageyama had foretold it.

Once, because my grades had gone up, Kageyama bluntly demanded an increase in his monthly fee or a bonus. My mother conferred with my grandfather, who despised and cursed Kageyama but in the end gave him the bonus he was looking for.

As soon as he came back to my room, Kageyama greedily tore open the envelope before my very eyes and counted the money. He then took the one thousand-yen notes one at a time, folded them small, and stuffed them into a purse that hung from a string around his neck.

Kageyama's lessons grew ever harsher after that.

On the day of Hashiguchi's funeral, something strange happened to me.

A bus brought my classmates from school to Hashiguchi's home in the Shibuya suburbs. Hashiguchi's father came from a noble family, and he managed several businesses, so his child's funeral was to be a grand affair. The guests filled the garden, and rows of people carrying burning sticks of incense continued to file past the whole time I, as a representative of the class, was reading the eulogy.

As the teacher instructed me, I read my long eulogy slowly, as solemnly as possible. At some point I happened to look up, and I saw Kageyama's face in the line of well-wishers.

At first I thought it was just someone who looked like him. After he had placed his incense, however, he looked at me for a second and smiled his ugly smile.

I wondered why Kageyama would be there and became confused. I lost my place in the eulogy and ended up skipping over whole chunks of it, finally reading just the last few lines.

It may have been that Kageyama heard from my mother where I was going to be and came to hear me read the eulogy. Or perhaps he was there in place of my parents, to light a stick of incense in their name. Neither of these things would have been unnatural. But in my mind, the image of the tutor Hashiguchi had detested like the Devil himself was now inextricably bound with the image of Kageyama.

I embraced the foolish fantasy that Hashiguchi's tutor had killed him, and that the tutor who had killed Hashiguchi was now looking for his next victim, and that search had led him to my house.

That year, more than any other, I was looking forward to New Year's.

From the time of the traditional Christmas party in the big hall of the Western annex, right through January 5, I would have no home lessons.

Our Christmas party had nothing to do with Christ's birth; it was just a year-end party at Christmas time. My father used any excuse to put on a show, and for the big party at the end of the year he always invited hundreds of guests, all imaginable kinds of people. The fir tree at the edge of the terrace was decorated as a Christmas tree right where it stood, and the entire ivy-covered Western wing was strung with lights.

In the two months since my home lessons had begun, I had not had a single chance to play in a sense that I would call playing, and so New Year's seemed more rapturous than ever.

I was able to eat and drink as I pleased, with no one to find fault with me. I received copious presents, and there was something else I looked forward to every year: it was the one night of the year that, with all my friends and relatives there, I was able to play to my heart's content, until the very end of the party.

The party began at dusk, and as the day drew slowly toward its close, the entire household was enveloped in an out-of-the-ordinary bustle and light. Until later that night when the party began to die and the guests trickled away one by one, the children played a huge game of hide-and-seek that used the entire estate from one end to the other.

A middle school-age cousin of mine was the first to be

"it." Her long hair was bound in a ponytail, and her school uniform made her pale face look especially beautiful.

I was thinking I wanted to hold her hand, and I let her catch me. The two of us became "it," and we ran around trying to catch the other kids. We searched everywhere, in both the main house and the Western annex, and ultimately the two of us, hands still entwined, entered the woods around the pond.

The forest on the far side of the pond was so deep that crows built nests there. By the light of the moon, we passed through the leaf-strewn cherry grove to a small man-made hill ringed by azalea plantings. I knew that the gazebo there would be an ideal hiding place.

"See, I told you! Somebody's here!" I whispered to my cousin in a low voice. Above the wooden panel that rose a few inches from the floor of the gazebo, I could see two heads facing the other way. My cousin and I approached, trying not to rustle the leaves.

As we reached the foot of the man-made hill, I pulled my cousin's hand close to me, because now I could see that the two shadows were not children. One was the silhouette of a man with a peaked cap pushed back on his head, moonlight flashing from his glasses when he turned to the side.

My cousin and I crept back to the azaleas.

After a while, we could see the two heads become one, and we could hear the sounds of lust. The man pushed the woman over, and they sank beneath the wooden panel at the base of the sliding doors, and the night air was filled with raw, fearsome groans. Then a porcelain-white leg flopped from behind the wooden panel to the outside air.

I became uncomfortable, anxious, and I started to stand up, but my cousin pulled me back.

"Shh. Quiet!"

As she strained her eyes in the darkness, my cousin's palms were sweaty. I was still not understanding anything, but

I could hear my own heart pounding deep in my eardrums.

The woman's voice changed from alarm to something like a female bird twittering. We could hear the man's breathing as well.

Quietly, my cousin pulled my hand to her chest. My fingertips could feel her fleshy, warm, damp skin. My cousin was not her usual self.

My thought at that point was that Kageyama was doing something evil to someone under cover of darkness, and that that magical power had somehow been projected onto my cousin.

Just as I was thinking he truly was the Devil, I sprang up and ran for my life. Behind me I could hear faint shrieks and cries of surprise.

My cousin and her family stayed until late in the night, when nearly all the other guests had left. Before climbing into the hired car, my cousin beckoned me into a dark corner by the main gate.

"I got some money. How about you?"

I shook my head, and my cousin heaved a sigh of sympathy.

"Well, I guess they didn't realize you were there too."

I could not grasp what my cousin was saying.

"You mean, Kageyama gave you money?"

"No!" she said, her eyes glistening in the darkness. "Auntie. So that I wouldn't tell anybody about what we saw."

She put her palm to her mouth as if in shock, but the gesture was a little theatrical.

Once the new year began, my depressing lessons resumed.

As usual, my father was seldom home. When he did come home, he was always so drunk he hardly even knew his name. The very air in the house seemed to turn somehow brutal. The various workers and maids who lived with us were often whispering among themselves, but if I got close their faces suddenly turned to smiles. My grandfather had always been imperturbable, but now he would lose his temper with my mother at the slightest little thing.

Clearly something about the household was beginning to change.

The decisive event took place before my eyes, one evening when a light snow was falling. Kageyama came to my room at the usual time, and as he was still making up his mind about whether or not to sit down, I could hear my grandfather coming down the hall.

"Might I have a word with you, tutor?"

His words had a sting to them, and my grandfather's face was not its usual color.

"I'm very sorry, but we were just about to begin the lesson. If you need to speak with me, after the lesson would be better," Kageyama said, looking at his watch. I felt as if he were using me as a shield. My grandfather grabbed him by the arm so violently I thought the chair would topple over and dragged him from the room.

From the main hallway I could hear my grandfather's angry shouting, and Kageyama's lower responses. Quietly I snuck from my room and hid behind a pillar. I wondered why my grandfather, confronting Kageyama in the hall, appeared to be only half his size.

I blinked repeatedly, not at my grandfather's sudden indignation, but in surprise at the unnatural contrast.

The main hallway was so long and straight that the papered window at the eastern end appeared to be a single dot of red. To the left and right were paper doors leading to tatami rooms and the crosspieces of glass doors looking out on the garden. The ceiling was an embossed lattice with the family crest. I thought it must be some sort of geometric optical illusion. For me, Kageyama's giant size suggested he was not human, and he seemed to look like the Devil in a strange guise.

As he grilled the towering Kageyama, my grandfather was so flustered he kept coughing. He had a persistent cough even at the best of times, but this was different.

My grandfather's thin body bent over double, and he held his kimono sleeve to his mouth. Suddenly a cry of pain burst from his throat, and he bent over backward from the waist. The pure white paper doors were sprayed with fresh blood, like a bouquet of flowers.

My grandfather fell on his backside, dumbfounded, and sat there cross-legged holding his two bloody hands open before his chest. Kageyama pressed his huge hands down on my grandfather's shoulders.

An ambulance took my grandfather to the hospital, and he didn't die until years later, but that day was the last time I ever saw him. He never returned to the house.

Until the day he spat up blood, my grandfather never told anyone about the sickness in his chest, because that was how courageous he was. For me, though, because I had more or less witnessed his attack, no amount of explanation from the doctor, and no amount of clinical disinfectant in every corner of the corridor, could persuade me that the attack had anything to do with tuberculosis or any other conventional illness.

There was no doubt in my mind that Kageyama had cast some sort of awful spell.

I had to tell someone about this. But all the people around me were absolutely powerless. My mother and father, as far as I could tell, were already under Kageyama's power.

There was no one else left on earth who would be able to grasp my terror at the prospect that every evening I would have to face Kageyama alone in this vast household, just the two of us.

Perhaps because my grandfather was now gone, the changes in the household became ever more extreme. After the demise of the patriarch, the Devil began to systematically devour the entire household, bit by bit.

The young people living on the second floor of the Western wing began to leave, one by one. Within just a month or two, the annex became an abandoned no-man's land. The servants in the main house as well packed their bags and left, roughly one a week.

With each passing day, Kageyama's presence within the rapidly disintegrating household seemed to grow.

Leaving me to study on my own, Kageyama would go to the Western annex and appropriate a rocking chair, into which he sank himself to spend time happily poring over human dissection diagrams. Sometimes he would gaze at the cherry grove, just beginning to show signs of pink, mumbling to himself some incantation that I could not understand.

Once, my father, apparently possessed by something or other, went on a rampage, smashing windows all over the house, and after that he never came back again. From then on, whenever he called on the telephone my mother's face would darken as she held the receiver. Ultimately, she would shriek and slam the receiver down.

In the end, our household consisted of just my mother, myself, our oldest maid, and one driver who took me back and forth to school.

And at some point Kageyama, if we are to include him among the human, began living in the otherwise abandoned Western annex.

As soon as my study hours were over, Kageyama would return to the Western annex, so quickly it seemed he was skating across the yard. When I turned out the lights in my room at ten, I would see my mother crossing the garden in the moonlight on unsteady legs, as if bewitched.

As the weather grew warmer, the garden too went wild.

One day, after making sure there was not a soul anywhere in the compound, I snuck into the Western annex. I climbed the dusty circular staircase to Kageyama's room.

In his room, the ivy-covered windows faced north, and there was a rotten odor. There were books written in some incomprehensible Western alphabet. On the floor so much dirty laundry and underwear were scattered about there was no place to step. On the bed, which had a human-shaped depression, lay one of my mother's small *tabi* socks.

Another day as spring vacation neared, I went to the museum in Ueno. My friends were in high spirits, but I felt nauseous the whole trip. Everything that day terrified me: the dried mummy heads, the taxidermy animals, the dinosaur bones, and the darkness of outer space, even the spans of time measured in tens of thousands and hundreds of thousands of years. I looked down a stairwell at a giant pendulum meant to prove the rotation of the earth, and I was finally overcome and had to get down on my hands and knees.

On the way home, the bus went around the back of the park and down a hill. I saw the name "Yanaka" on a placard on a utility pole. That was where Kageyama used to live, but it didn't seem like the sort of place that would have a lot of boarding houses for students. For all I could see, the only things there were old temples and gravestones and wooden Buddhist memorial tablets.

All I could think about was that I needed to ask someone for help. When we got back to school and were dismissed, I went right away to a church that stood beside the wooded lane near the school.

The teachers at school were always telling us that if we had troubles or regrets we couldn't tell anyone about, we could always go to church and confess. Of course none of the pupils ever did any such thing, but I was so deeply tormented I decided that that's what I had to do.

A nun was cleaning, and I asked her if the priest was

there. Until the priest arrived, I sat in a pew in front and prayed. As I sat there mumbling some Biblical text I knew by heart, I grew very sad and started to cry.

I was a very lucky boy. My entire life I had been untouched by sickness or poverty. There was no reason on earth I should be crying, and the fact that I was crying over something like this made me think there must be something wrong with me. But just looking at the mute figure of the body of Christ, the tears came to my eyes.

The priest, clad in his vestments, put his arms around my shoulders, and I clung to him and bawled like a baby.

"The Devil is in my house. He's pretending to be a college student, my tutor, but really he's the Devil."

The priest did his best to calm me down, and then he appeared to be thinking.

"I think...I think that maybe you've been studying too hard. There's still time before the exams, though, so why don't you try to spend a little more time playing?"

"That's not it. My grandfather spat up blood, and my father went crazy, and our whole household is scattered all over the place, and now...my mother is being tormented every night."

The priest raised an eyebrow for an instant.

"What do you mean, 'tormented'?"

"The Devil torments my mother. He takes her to the gazebo in the garden or to an empty room, and my mother cries as if she's suffering. It's as if he's riding a horse, and then he squeezes her throat, or acts like he's going to break her arms and legs."

"Hmmm. But your mother hasn't been injured?"

The priest was confounded. I thought to myself that an elementary school priest wouldn't be powerful enough for an exorcism.

"I'm sure he's going to kill her."

"I wouldn't worry about that. Everything will be all right."

"How do you know?"

"The Lord Jesus protects you and your mother."

I did not feel the least bit better. That my household was under attack by the Devil was a grave truth, and I did not think God's power was protecting us.

"So what do I have to do to drive the Devil away? I don't know the first thing about this."

The priest thought for a while, and then he searched in the pocket of his vestments and brought out a little cross.

"I will give this to you. Even the Devil himself is a servant of the Lord. To drive the Devil away from you, you don't have to cry out the name of Jesus, you don't have to make the sign of the cross, you don't have to read the Gospels. If the Devil tries to do something evil to you, just hold on tight to this crucifix and stare him down. And say this: 'You are the Devil. You cannot defeat me.'"

Hearing that, my heart grew a little lighter. On the way home from the church, I repeated the spell the priest had taught me, over and over.

The next day, my mother was summoned to the school. I have no idea what they talked about. In the car on the way home, my mother said not a word and didn't so much as glance at my face.

The cherry blossoms were falling before we really had a chance to have a proper cherry blossom-viewing party. Just about that time, Hashiguchi's mother came to pay us a visit.

She said she should have come sooner, but she was calling on each of the families that had attended her son's funeral, one by one, and the process was dragging on.

She held her head up straight and kept her young, beautiful face trained on me.

"You must be going into fifth grade soon. Minus one of your rivals."

Why in the world would she say something like that, I

thought to myself, feeling uncomfortable. I was reminded of how Hashiguchi's mother had meticulously stuffed his tiny coffin full of his textbooks and reference books.

"Do you have your eye on Azabu or Kaisei? Or maybe the Teachers' College Junior High School?"

Without a moment's hesitation, I blurted out something completely unexpected. "I plan to go to the local public high school."

"Why ever would you do something like that? You're such a good student!"

"Just normal would be fine with me."

The air in the sitting room suddenly turned chilly.

Just as the grandfather clock struck five, Kageyama appeared. He had become just like one of the family, entering through the front door without announcing his arrival and coming down the long hallway with his sliding gait.

As he passed the open door of the sitting room, Hashiguchi's mother let out a hysterical cry of surprise.

"Tutor! What are you doing here?"

"Ah, how nice to see you again."

With those few words, Kageyama made it clear he had no interest in having anything to do with Hashiguchi's mother, and he passed on by.

From just that tiny snippet of conversation, my mother and I understood immediately what was going on, and we looked at each other and closed our mouths. We contemplated Kageyama's big fat lie.

After an uncomfortable silence, Hashiguchi's mother spoke, the distaste obvious in her voice. "It may be a little late to be warning you like this, but you should keep an eye on that tutor."

That gave me goose bumps. My mother, flustered, responded, "Oh? What do you mean by that exactly?"

"Well, even Tokyo University students come in all stripes."

At that moment, I suddenly remembered Hashiguchi's warning. *"Lately he's been tormenting my mother. He must be the Devil."*

I could picture Hashiguchi sitting under a ginkgo tree sucking on his inhaler, saying those words, his voice fading to a whisper. I was sure of it.

I will never forget the day the Devil showed his true colors.

It was a midsummer afternoon, and the cicadas were buzzing noisily in the increasingly forlorn-looking cherry orchard. My mother and I had placed rattan pillows in the middle of the big reception room, which had a nice breeze, and we were taking a nap. We were listless, but not because of the heat, and not out of boredom. All the life had gone out of us, both my mother and me, and no matter what we thought of doing it was too much trouble.

The maid and the driver had left us at the end of the school term, and my mother and I now lived huddled together by ourselves in the unimaginably huge compound, like bugs in a torrid desert.

My mother let out a little snore. I was under the same blanket and clutched it to my belly, gazing aimlessly out at the garden as the afternoon wound down.

Watching the shimmering heat rise from the pond, I began to doze off, when all of a sudden my mother sat bolt upright with a shriek.

"What have you done? You! What have you done?"

I hadn't done anything. But from my mother's bare foot, from the tips of her toes, fresh blood had dripped on the tatami. Both her nightgown and her *yukata* robe were stained bright red.

The two of us ran to the paper sliding dividers and gazed across the broad expanse of the reception room. From somewhere in the shadow of one of the dividers we could hear a sound like scratching on the tatami mat. We focused our listening, and the sound seemed to grow louder, like something digging or scratching at a wooden pillar or one of the paper-covered dividers. Just a short ways away was a paper divider covered with a landscape painting, and it was shaking audibly.

My mother and I slid backwards on our backsides toward the display alcove. In my mind, I was imagining that a knife-wielding burglar had snuck into our home and cut my mother's foot.

My mother picked up the rattan pillow, took aim at the rattling paper divider, and let it fly. At that moment, I heard a loud scratching, as if something was clambering up the pillar. A deep black shadow was plastered across the gaps in the transom.

Transfixed by the shining stare of two eyes, my mother crouched on the tatami. Perhaps alarmed by her shrieking, the shadow fled to the other side of the paper divider. I watched its eyes as the big, black beast ran through the room, from one paper-covered divider to the next.

Mother and I froze, unable to move, as if we were bound hand and foot.

"Was that...a rat?"

"No way. It was lots bigger. It was even bigger than a cat or a dog."

What I could not bring myself to say was that I thought it was the Devil. I gripped tightly the cross that hung at my chest.

On my mother's toe there was a huge wound, shaped like a person's teeth. Leaving my mother collapsed where she was, I ran terrified into the hallway. In my hand I had a big broom, and I bent over as I walked down the hall. The house never seemed so large to me as it did at that moment. It was a maze with no horizon as far as the eye could see, just a complicated hallway with myriad rooms.

I looked into each room, one by one, until I reached the

kitchen at the north end of the house. It was an earthen-floored kitchen, with sinks and counters as big as a restaurant's. It was spacious, with one area floored with gleaming blackened wood, reflecting the long history of the house, and another tatami area at a slightly higher level. At one time there had been both cooks and chefs and a whole flock of maids standing there, working. The unfamiliar quiet was almost more than I could bear.

The Devil was sitting in the gloomy center of the wood-floored area, its body curled up in a ball. The dust glittered and danced in the stripe of light that entered through the chimney hole in the ceiling, and directly below that sat the Devil in its foul, heavy, black, hairy form.

If this was not some hallucination on my part, it was much bigger than an ordinary human. It had two twisted horns, a deeply wrinkled face like a very old person, and black wings that gleamed as if oiled.

I gripped the cross beneath my shirt and strove with all my might to remember the spell the priest had taught me.

But the Devil spoke first, as if to silence my voice. "Just what do you think you're doing? I will devour your grandfather, your father, and your mother. Not one will be left, and I will drag you all to Hell."

At last I was able to move my frozen lips. "You are the Devil. I...I..."

"Hmm. You are what? Are you trying to say that I cannot defeat you? What can you do to me? You're just a lousy little kid who knows nothing of how the world works, who just sits at a desk reading and writing. I will destroy you all! You and all the rest of the household will fall to Hell!"

The Devil opened his fiery mouth and laughed, as if to intimidate me, and noisily and impatiently spread his gigantic black wings. A dizzyingly foul odor filled the air, and the Devil slipped out through a gap in the door to the back garden.

The very next day, I was taken to the home of my mother's relatives.

Nothing was said to me in advance. A motorized cargo trike came to pick me up and take me to my uncle's home in the suburbs.

What my plainspoken uncle told me was that our family business was in difficulties, and that both my father and mother had to go away for a while. I did not know where away was. Neither did I want to know.

The luggage rack of the motorized trike held just a few of my things.

We bumped along the pebble path, and I turned back to look for the window of my mother's room. In the fading sunlight striking the gabled front gate stood my mother like a cast-off shell, waving her white hand.

In the old farmhouse, I was finally able to breathe easily.

But this was a cowardly respite, filled with loneliness and despair. As I finally relaxed, bit by bit I began to talk about what had happened to me. I did not shy away from discussing my encounter with the Devil.

My aunt and uncle listened intently to what I had to say, and from time to time they would sigh in reproach at my mother and father's conduct. My aunt and uncle had had little to do with our household in the past. Once I talked back to them, asking why they said such things if they didn't really know what had happened. My uncle thought for a bit and answered me, "People can be so stinking rich, but when it comes right down to it, they don't think of anyone but themselves. This is a pain you must not ever forget, your whole life long."

My uncle said I must be terribly tired and should give up studying for a while, and during summer vacation he bought an old used TV for me.

When it came time for me to start the second school term, I was sent to a public school that was surrounded by fields of tea bushes.

At that school there was no church and no priest, just an old wooden building and a teacher who looked like a pro wrestler and called me by just my first name. It was the strangest thing I'd ever seen, but that teacher would stand at his rostrum in his running shirt, looking like Toyonobori himself, and entertain us all by waving his arms that looked like tree trunks, making a funny sound.

At lunchtime I would try to study, and he would come up to me, blowing on a whistle, and tell me I had to play softball instead.

My customary greeting was to say "Good day!" but everyone laughed at the way I put the accent on "day." I still felt like I was different from the other kids, but nobody would leave me alone. Like some weak-willed religious convert, I became just like one of them, without even having to tread upon the icons of my former faith.

At recess and in gym class, I had to endure the others' derisive sniggers. But the first time I shagged an outfield fly ball without dropping it, cheers went up from all around, both in the field and from the windows of the school building. Just as if I were some sort of baseball star, I clutched the winning ball to my chest and ran all the way from center field to home plate, crying the whole way.

Under an autumn sky bigger than any I had ever seen, I was firmly protected by the good will of people, not gods. Over time, I began to recover my spirit.

Just once I returned to my real home, around the time the mountains surrounding the school started to turn the color of gold.

A buyer had been found for the house, and I was to go back to claim just the things I needed.

Given how great my terror had been, it was a wonder that I felt none that day. On the contrary, I felt that this would close that chapter of my life for good.

The long gate of the house was closed in a way that seemed to suggest it would never open again, and it was sealed with an official-looking sheet of paper. At the coppery gray-green side gate, which led to the Western annex, loitered a number of unsavory-looking men.

My uncle accepted a bundle of keys from a big ugly man and drove the cargo trike down the pebble path. The autumn colors of the estate, a brilliant red and orange, enveloped me. Above the cherry grove hung the large, late afternoon sun.

At the main gate crouched a silhouette.

"Ah, I see your tutor is here," my uncle said, hesitating a bit. "Your mother must have told him we were coming."

Without understanding the import of these words, I looked at his face. My uncle pressed his lips together, as if he realized he had said too much.

In my pocket I gripped the cross. The trike stopped at the gate, and Kageyama stood up, stretching his tall body upward like some sort of mechanical toy. Removing his peaked cap, he bowed. The look on my uncle's face was one of obvious discomfort. Kageyama asked how I was doing, and my uncle gave no sign of response.

The main door of the house was padlocked on the outside. My uncle unlocked and opened the door. The dark interior of the house was painted with red stripes of light like flames.

"It's dirty. We can leave our shoes on," my uncle said, stepping up to the main floor in his traditional split-toed canvas shoes.

The main room was wet inside, even though the rain shutters were closed, and the room was filled with an odor that made me nauseous. Kageyama put his uniformed arm over my shoulder. I freed myself and ran after my uncle, who was already walking down the dark corridor.

"Uncle, we should open the rain shutters."

"You want to let in some air?"

As we went down the long corridor, we ourselves opened all the rain shutters, a job that used to be done every morning and evening by all the servants of the household in a great bustle.

"About halfway should do it. We're going to have to close them again."

Now that the shutters were open the late afternoon sun came flooding in, and the red-dyed sumacs and cherry trees were visible beyond the garden.

At that instant, we stopped what we were doing and stood stock-still. The entire expanse of the great reception room was covered with dead rats, piles and piles of them, so many there was no place to step. The tatami was slathered with dried black blood. The entire one hundred-mat room was covered with dried rat heads and limbs and organs, from one end to the other.

"Gosh, with the house all closed up like this, they just ate each other to death. Leave them be." My uncle stepped down wearily into the garden and headed for the Western annex.

Thus was the demise of the house in which I was born and grew up. Kageyama and I stood still for a while in the red light. Birds were twittering in the treetops, and in the distance we could hear a bell tolling vespers.

Gripping the cross in my pocket, I blurted out, "You did this! You ate them all and left them lying all around! You ate them!"

The shadows that stretched long across the lake of blood hung like folded wings.

"What's wrong with you? Say something! You ate them all, and now you have nothing left to eat! You must be so hungry you can't even think of anything nasty to say!"

Kageyama just stood there, hanging his head and biting his lip. I was not afraid of him. I thrust the cross at his face and said, "You are the Devil. But you cannot defeat me!"

Kageyama lifted his pale face and moved his mouth several

times as if to speak. I thought the spell had been successful.

"You are the Devil. But you cannot defeat me!"

Just then I heard an awful scratching. The same sound as on that day.

"Something...is here!" Kageyama said, frightened. We walked across the room, feeling the awful corpses beneath our feet.

Kageyama and I walked past several rooms and peered into the very last one, and there, on top of even more piled-up dead rats, we saw something terrible.

There, holding down one trapped rat with its front paw, and gnawing on another, head first, was a giant rat the size of a small dog.

Still crunching on the bones, the monster stared at us. It must have been very old, and its fur was very black and gleaming. Its ears stood up like a rabbit's, and its face was deeply wrinkled like an ancient one. It had a long tail like a snake, which it waved as if trying to intimidate us.

Kageyama screamed and stomped his foot, and at that, with incredible agility, its prey still in its mouth, the monster rat ran off somewhere.

After we stood there for some time, Kageyama fell deflated to his knees.

"I never meant for it to be like this...but as you can see, I was not the only one at fault. You see that now, don't you?"

"You are the Devil! You are the Devil!"

But it wasn't so. The thing I had believed to be the Devil must actually have been that giant rat. And if that were the case, what did that make Kageyama?

I was confused, but my lips continued to mumble, "You are the Devil. You are the Devil."

"Look at me. I am apologizing to you."

Placing his hands on the dried blood, Kageyama bent his forehead down at my feet.

My memory stops there.

Perhaps what happened after that simply no longer had any bearing on my life.

Happily, the devils that had plagued me until then later died like ordinary mortals, and I never saw them again.

High-rise condominiums were eventually built on the site where the house I was born in had once stood. Beside the entrance stands an old cherry tree, like some forgotten article in a lost and found.

In
Tsunohazu

Kyoichi Nukui's farewell party took place one hot evening past the middle of July.

If the party was livelier than most, it was not because
the participants were congratulating him on his reassignment
from sales chief of the parent company to general manager
of the Rio de Janeiro office, but nearly the opposite. The
announcement was out of season, and out of sympathy for
his sudden demotion and because of the urgent appeals of his
team members on the project that he was being made to take
the fall for, the partygoers emitted a buoyant enthusiasm.

Forty-six years old. Kyoichi Nukui had been born in the
last year of the baby boom, and he had no shortage of rivals.
Practically speaking, for a trading company man to be sent
abroad at this point in his career was the end of the line.
The Rio de Janeiro office's primary responsibility was buying
coffee beans, a specialized field, the kind of job where experi-
enced branch managers generally live out their days in exile.

The send-off party was held in the rented banquet room
of a hotel, and the comedians among the younger staff members were brazenly calling it "Nukui's funeral."

More than a few people were secretly gloating about the
setback suffered by this particular Tokyo University gradu-
ate and former success story. The goodbye party attracted a
large number of revelers, and people were giving him farewell

presents of cash, which seemed more like hush money.

As though to prove this, the guests departed like an ebbing tide at the end of the two-hour buffet, leaving in the lobby only Nukui and three of his former employees who had somehow emerged unscathed from the incident for which he alone had taken the blame.

In the six months since that project had been disbanded, Nukui had aged ten years. No trace was left of the gifted expert in food imports who had been successfully climbing the trading company's career ladder.

His pudgy body was that of an indolent middle-aged man who had let himself go. His thinning hair suggested a certain shabbiness, and his thick eyeglasses were smudged with grease.

If Nukui had his druthers, he would have liked to go straight home. But he also knew he had to comfort his three comrades, who were feeling the pain of responsibility. When he thought of his wife sitting childless and alone in the immaculately tidy condominium, he knew he didn't want to arrive home in his current tipsy state.

"What do you say, boss, how about we go to Golden Gai? We haven't been there in ages," said Oda, who was three years Nukui's junior. When they were young men, the two of them had often gone together to Golden Gai.

As trading company employees grow older, however, they tend to socialize in classier bars and restaurants, and these two had long since lost any connection to the cheap dives in which they had drunk and told each other of their dreams.

"Golden Gai? Ah, you mean Golden Gai in Tsunohazu?"

"That's right. Tsunohazu. I haven't heard that name in years."

As they walked through the lobby, their younger colleague inquired, "Tsunohazu? What's that? A bar?"

"No, no. Once upon a time the district we now call Kabuki-cho was known as Tsunohazu. We used to call it

'Golden Gai in Tsunohazu,' didn't we, Oda?"

"Haa," Oda said, but there was no emotion in his voice. It was only then that Nukui understood why he had suddenly made this suggestion.

Over one hundred people had attended the party, and all of them had by now moved on to their favorite little watering holes somewhere to continue drinking. He wouldn't want to run into any of them at the usual places, where they would be reciting their litany of gossip.

From the hotel lobby they could see the company headquarters building against the night sky above the new city center. Ten years ago, the company had moved here from the increasingly overcrowded Otemachi district of Tokyo.

Looking up at the skyscraper fortress—which in all likelihood he would never see again—Nukui heaved the sigh of an old man.

It was the kind of evening when the damp heat clung to your body like festering seaweed. As they left the little bar in Golden Gai, Nukui got a schnozful of bad air and puked into the plants on the promenade.

This was rare for Nukui, who thought to himself he must really be under a lot of stress. The bar had been one familiar to him from way back, though it had changed hands. The things Nukui had been unable to say came up with his vomit.

"The three of you must never again speak my name at the office."

Oda, who had been gently massaging Nukui's back, suddenly stopped.

"You are salarymen, and you just have to stay in step. You can all drum your own drums and blow your own flutes and clap your hands in rhythm, but as long as you all remain on the beat, everything will be okay. It would be out of step for you to be talking, even out of carelessness, about the decrepit old branch manager who got shipped off to Rio. Got it? Promise me, or I won't be able to live with myself."

Nukui started to walk on down the promenade, leaving his subordinates trailing in his wake.

"Listen to me. You don't have to see me off tomorrow. Just my wife and I, like we're going off on our honeymoon. Leave us alone."

The three subordinates made no attempt to follow him.

In his drunken state, Nukui now thought everything would be all right. For the past twenty-three years, everything had simply gone too smoothly for him. Pride goeth before a fall. His childhood years had been humble, but then he had gone to Tokyo University, entered an elite trading company, and for a fleeting moment he had been given a taste of glory. It had been a miracle.

From Yasukuni-dori he telephoned his wife.

"Hi. It's me. I'm on my way home."

"Have you had something to eat? There's nothing here in the house."

"It's fine. I'm a little drunk. Have you eaten?"

"I had take-out a little while ago. The sushi shop is still open, but that's no good for you."

"Well, I guess I don't have any choice but sushi though."

"No, I can get you something from the convenience store. And breakfast for tomorrow."

Nukui had never fought with his wife, whom he had known since childhood. They were actually second cousins and had grown up together like siblings. If anything, they knew each other too well.

Nukui's wife had been taken aback by the recent announcement. It had not been anything for them to fight about, but he wished she had said something.

It was the middle of the night, but you wouldn't know it given the ceaseless flow of people streaming between Kabuki-cho and the east exit of Shinjuku Station. In the fantastic, windless night, people swarmed like some kind of tropical fish.

To Nukui's inebriated eyes the neon lights were explosive.

His glasses were damp, and the red, blue, and yellow lights blurred together. He stood his ground firmly, but just then he saw something strange on the far side of Yasukuni-dori.

"Dad…"

Without thinking, he sprang out into the road, but the sound of horns brought him to his senses, and he stopped and squinted to see better.

"Dad…Dad…"

In front of the rolled-down shutters of a shop, he could see his father, wearing a white Panama hat, a hemp suit, and a shirt open at the collar. He was looking warily around him and asking something of the people passing by.

"Dad! I'm over here! Look over here!"

All the hustle and bustle drowned out his voice. His father was looking for him.

"Dad!" Nukui called again, but his father disappeared.

The light changed. Thrashing his way through the throng of people, Nukui finally managed to get across the avenue. The Kabuki-cho bus stop, its lights out. He was sure this was where his father had been.

"Was a middle-aged man just here?" he asked some young men seated on the guardrail. They had pompadour hairstyles and dangling pierced earrings. They laughed at him.

"We just missed each other. He was wearing a Panama hat and a white suit. He seemed to be looking for me, but he didn't see me."

"Don't know what you're talking about," they answered him curtly. "First of all, there's nothing about a middle-aged man worth paying attention to around here. If it's some homeless guy you're looking for, there's a bunch of them over there.

Secondly, don't remember seeing any white suit."

They were pointing to the bunch of bums lying in front of the shop shutters and laughing. Then they looked back at Nukui and laughed again. He was the one who stood out at this hour.

Homeless. Nukui felt a shiver. He had often wondered if his father's life had come to that. When a large number of homeless had first taken up residence in the pedestrian tunnels at the west exit of Shinjuku Station, he had taken an old photograph of his father and walked among them, asking questions.

The homeless of Kabuki-cho had been sleeping well in the happy season.

"I am looking for Ichiro Nukui. From Nakano-ku. Ichiro Nukui. Does anyone here know anyone by that name?"

From inside a cardboard box came the response, "Shut up, you drunk!"

There was no doubt in his mind that the man he had just seen, looking around him, was his father. Wait, no, something didn't fit. The man he had seen looked just like his father had when he left. And he was not an old man.

It must have been a drunken hallucination. Nukui looked back across the road.

There stood a row of somber ginkgo trees, widely spaced. The name of the bus stop had been changed from Tsunohazu to Kabuki-cho. Other than that, the neighborhood looked much the same as it always had.

Nearly forty years had passed since that summer when he was eight years old. But he could remember it as if it were yesterday.

·2·

"Kyoichi! You want some sushi?" Kyoichi's father said to him as he got off the bus at the Tsunohazu stop, pushing back the brim of his Panama hat and looking up at the evening sky.

"Dad, I heard Nagashima from Rikkyo University is going to sign up with the Giants. Is that true?"

"Well now, I wouldn't know about that."

As they crossed the intersection, hand in hand, Kyoichi was trying to think of things to talk about with his dad. In his other hand, the father carried the son's satchel as if it held a bomb.

Once they were across the street, Kyoichi's father looked around the area like he was through being bothered, then took off his glasses and wiped the sweat from his face. He seemed unable to make up his mind about something.

Kyoichi finally brought himself to say the lines he had been thinking in the bus all the way from Nakano. "So Dad, here's what I think. It's okay with me if a new mom comes to live with us. That woman, she's pretty, don't you think? Younger and prettier than Mom was. All right, Dad? That's what I think you should do."

It was pure theater. His dad had brought the woman to the house several times, and Kyoichi had never once thought she was pretty. She had big eyes like a raccoon, and her lips curved strangely. She had a habit of clucking her tongue whenever her eyes met Kyoichi's, and she would turn her face away.

As soon as he had spoken his terrible lines, Kyoichi shut his eyes and apologized to his dead mother.

"Is that so? To tell the truth, though, she's not that crazy about you."

"Why not? I never did anything to her."

"No, it's not that. It's just that she doesn't particularly like kids." As Ichiro spoke these words, he looked back at the east exit of the concrete structure of Shinjuku Station.

"So, how about it, shall we have some sushi? You must be hungry."

"No, I'm not."

Eating sushi always reminded him of last rites somehow, and he couldn't stand it. If ever he ate sushi, all he could think was that would be the end.

"So Dad, where is she right now? Is she waiting for you someplace?"

Somewhere deep behind his eyeglasses, Ichiro's eyes widened for just an instant, but then right away they turned a sad color.

"Why do you ask?"

"No reason. I just felt like it."

Across the back of Ichiro's hemp suit a sweat stain was spreading.

They entered the sushi shop that was right by the bus stop, and his father told him to go ahead and order whatever he wanted to eat.

Kyoichi was unfamiliar with the ritual of sitting on the high stools at the counter and ordering different kinds of sushi. As he sat there in silence, his father ordered for him things that he thought a child would like. He was being more considerate than usual.

Kyoichi thought that if he cried, he might still be able to change his father's mind. But the boy also had his pride.

In contrast to the uproar in his heart, the sushi was melt-in-the-mouth good, and it felt sad.

"Kyoichi, just always make sure you're good at your studies," said his father between sips of beer, like some kind of last wish. "I was never able to keep up in school. Between my apprenticeship and the army, I was never able to, even if I wanted to. So even now, people find it easy to make me look stupid."

"You're not stupid, Dad." What he really wanted to say was, *You're not stupid enough to walk out on your own kid, are you?* He had no idea, however, whether his father would understand.

"Actually, I am. Stupid enough to run my company into the ground. The truth is, I never really had any interest in going into business. I'm not that brave, either. I should have been a salaryman."

"So why don't you just be a salaryman then?"

"To be a salaryman, first you have to finish college. But then you get Sundays off, you only have to work a half-day on Saturdays, and you don't have to work too hard to make your money."

Some mournful *enka* music was playing on the radio. Ichiro didn't eat any sushi, he just drank beer. And then he worked himself up to saying something brave, something frightening.

"Kyoichi, I have to go soon. There's something I have to take care of. You go to your uncle's, in Yodobashi. Take the bus from Tsunohazu, two stops. You know the way, right?"

It was actually Ichiro's cousin's house and not far from Shinjuku.

"Yat-chan and Kumi-chan are also on summer vacation, so you guys can just have a good time until I can come get you."

Kyoichi was so shocked he forgot to keep chewing his sushi. Finally he remembered to swallow.

"You'll come get me later tonight?"

His father hesitated before answering.

"You see, there's some work I have to do. If I can't come get you tonight, you can just spend the night there."

"It's okay. I think I'll just go home and wait for you there. You can come home as late as you like."

He wanted to add, *please, please,* but his voice failed him.

"No, that's not going to work. Just go to your uncle's. I'll give you a call."

And at that, his father put a whole lot of money in his hand, as allowance, and some bus tickets.

At the Tsunohazu bus stop, his father said goodbye.

"I'll just wait for you here, Dad. I'll wait as long as it takes. Just come back here."

"Aren't you a stubborn one. What I'm saying is, I don't know if I'll be able to come back tonight or not."

"I'll just wait here for you. I'll wait until the last bus. Just be sure to come back."

Just maybe, he had gotten through. In the twilit street, his father leaned over and hugged him around the shoulders.

"Yeah, you should become a salaryman. Make sure you be good at your studies and get a good job at a big company."

Kyoichi wanted to yell, *Yeah, and then someday maybe I won't have to dump my kid in the street!*

And then his father left.

Kyoichi waited and waited at the Tsunohazu bus stop for his father, though he knew he was not coming back.

It was the kind of damp night when the white light of the streetlamps seemed ready to absorb the fuzzy blue and red of the neon. At first, Kyoichi stared at the passing cars. Before long he remembered he had a piece of chalk in the pocket of his short pants. He used it to draw a picture of a Zero fighter plane on the sidewalk.

All around the bus stop, Zeros and Battleship Yamatos and entire battalions appeared, but his father did not.

People working in the restaurant scolded him. When he apologized for drawing pictures in front of the restaurant, one of them asked him, rather nicely, what he was doing there at that time of night.

"Waiting for my father," he said, biting his lip at the pain of his own words. He knew his father wasn't coming back. But he didn't want to be an orphan, so he saw no alternative but to wait right there.

As the night went on, the restaurant closed, and the restaurant worker came out, singing a rockabilly song quietly to himself, and scrubbed Kyoichi's pictures from the pavement with a stiff broom. As he started to lower the shutter, he threw a cold look in Kyoichi's direction, but then he went inside and came out with a chilled bottle of Ramune soda pop.

Many buses came and went, each with fewer and fewer passengers. With each passing bus, Kyoichi's heart grew more hollow. By the time a completely empty bus came, his heart too was empty.

Then came the last bus to Ogikubo. There were only a few passengers, and they all got off.

"Last bus! Hey kid, this is the last bus! You okay?" the bus driver asked, bending forward as he pulled the handle of the folding door. Before getting on the bus, Kyoichi looked around Tsunohazu one last time.

The lights of most of the shops were already out, and the alley cats were starting to come out.

His "uncle" in Yodobashi was a maker of wooden bathtubs. His aunt was waiting for him at the bus stop. She said she had been waiting for two hours, ever since his father had called.

"I'm sorry, auntie."

"You shouldn't have to apologize." And that was all she said.

Kyoichi had a pretty good idea of what was happening to him, but he didn't want anyone to know how much he understood, so he played dumb.

"Auntie, I heard that Nagashima from Rikkyo University is going to play for the Giants next year. You think it's true?"

"Hmm, I have no idea. When we get to the house, ask your uncle."

His aunt's hand reminded him of the warmth of his mother's hand.

They descended the Naruko slope and found Kyoichi's uncle drinking a beer on a platform in front of his workshop.

His two second cousins, Yasuo and Kumiko, were kneeling beside him playing with sparklers.

"Look, Kyoichi's here!" Kumiko said, running toward him in her nightgown, her wooden *geta* sandals making a clatter.

"Kyoichi! They say you're coming to live with us!"

"What are you talking about?" Kyoichi's aunt responded in a loud voice.

"Dad said so. Kyoichi's mom died, and his dad has to go someplace, so Kyoichi's going to be my big brother."

When little Kumi-chan gave him a hug, only then did Kyoichi hold his forearm to his brow and cry.

·3·

"Don't worry about it. You must've just had some bad sake. That's...you can't help it."

Squaring her shoulders against the window in the spartan living room, Kumiko smiled. For Nukui to drink a beer with his wife was a rare occasion. Kumiko had spent her whole life in Shinjuku and looked no younger than she was, but the new skyscrapers filling the window somehow suited her.

"You think? But I felt like I was seeing him so clearly."

"But think about it for a minute. A Panama hat and a hemp suit? Who wears things like that these days?"

"That's exactly why I think it's so strange. I'm sure I was not mistaken. Of course whether or not it was my father is a separate question, but I'm sure I saw a man of that description walking down the other side of the street. I'm sure I saw him."

"A hallucination, an illusion. It does seem sad though. And by the way, how are we going to sleep in this apartment tonight, sir?"

Looking around, Nukui saw that the bedroom was empty. Not even a bed.

"I'm so sorry. The new people want to move in as soon as we're out of here. So I got rid of the bed today. Today was the only collection day for oversize garbage."

They had been lucky to get a good price for their condo at a time like this. Nukui's wife was being more considerate of the buyers than was strictly necessary.

"Kind of a waste, don't you think? The new people could have used that bed."

"Actually, Kyoichi," Kumiko said. "Think about this from their point of view. No matter what you might think about other furniture, a bed is a bed…"

"You have a point there."

It had been a double bed that they bought with monthly installments when they were still newlyweds. What Kyoichi now saw as a waste was because twenty years of memories had just gone out the door.

How was it that the two of them, who had grown up practically as brother and sister, had fallen in love? Kumiko had gone to a two-year college, and something her father had said around that time, half in jest, had actually come to pass before they knew it.

On that bed, now thrown away, the two of them had clumsily explored the rites of love, and over time they had cherished it.

"They said this is going to be the child's room."

Whenever Nukui heard his wife say the word *child*, he felt a chill. He had never made her a mother. In his own eyes, that was his only sin as far as she was concerned.

"How about the futon?" he asked, changing the subject.

"Oh, uh, promise you won't be mad at me?"

"Okay, I won't be mad at you."

"My brother came to get the TV and the living room set. And I just gave him the futon with all that. I mean, he had the car here already and everything, so I just gave it to him. I didn't think about it until after he left. It was stupid of me."

They both laughed.

"You weren't thinking, and neither was your brother! You're two of a kind!"

"Two of a kind? We are siblings, after all…"

As soon as she said it, Kumiko tried to think of something else she could say, to take her words back. She knelt where she was and hung her head.

"I'm sorry, Kyoichi."

"Huh? Why?"

"Because I talk too much, and I always say things I shouldn't. Things that might hurt you. I try to be careful."

Ever since they were children, Kyoichi had been aware of Kumiko's thoughtfulness. When he thought that now they would be crossing the seas and his wife would grow old still choosing her words carefully, Nukui couldn't bear it.

"I wonder why your father never put me in his family register?"

"I think it's because he always believed that someday your father would come back."

"But he never did." As soon as Nukui had spat out those words, he felt a tightness in his chest. The only time he had ever cried about what his father had done was on that night he had left him at the bus stop. He pressed his fingers to his eyelids and felt himself growing old.

Kumiko put her arms around his shoulders.

"Hey, hey there. You seem to be kind of on edge. But if my parents had adopted you, you and I could never have gotten married."

"I always wanted to call your father my father. Your mother my mother. You and your brother too, my sister and brother. Whenever I called any of you by your names, it made me feel like some kind of burden."

"You were never any sort of burden to us. My father and mother were always proud of you, until the day they died, weren't they? We were all proud of you."

When Nukui's admission to Tokyo University was announced, the entire family had gone to Hongo. No other newly accepted student could claim that. Looking at the expressions on the other family members' faces, Nukui felt he had been a long-term freeloader.

"Kyoichi, it may sound strange for me to be saying this now, but I want you to call me Kumiko, and not Kumi-chan. From now on."

"I'd be embarrassed. Why do you want me to do that?"

"Well, we'll be going someplace where no one knows us, and that's what I'd like you to do. Okay? You can do that, right?"

Whatever had he done to deserve her kindness, Kyoichi thought to himself. It must be something inherited.

When he was in middle school, on the school roster his address was recorded as "c/o Horiuchi." He hated this and told his uncle he would like to change his family name. He didn't exactly ask his uncle to adopt him, but it boiled down to the same thing.

"I never knew that. Did that really happen?"

"What do you think your father said then?"

"Hmm. I don't know. 'Stupid idiot! You think I'm going to go to all that bother' or something like that..."

"Unh-unh. He was working, planing some planks for a tub, and he picked up a scrap of wood and made me a name-plate for the front of the house. He used a magic marker and wrote 'Kyoichi Nukui' in really clumsy letters. And he said, 'How about it? Now we don't need any c/o.'"

"Aha! That nameplate is still there, on the house. I wonder if my brother ever noticed."

"There's no way he's never noticed. He just hasn't taken it down. He's very conscientious too."

"But..." Kumiko started to say as she let her hair down, as if she'd just thought of something. She laid her head on her husband's shoulder. The tempo of her quiet breathing matched the flashing of the red lights on the skyscrapers that filled the view from the window.

"I wonder why Dad never put you in the family register. I mean, if you asked him to."

"Well, that must have been because my dad…" And as he said the word *dad*, Nukui became filled with emotion. "Because he thought my dad would be coming back. That's the only way I can understand it."

"Or maybe because he wanted to match up the two of us."

"Hmm. You may be onto something. That may be it."

"I'm sure he never wanted to let you go. If you married me, you would be his son that way. A brilliant plan. And then…" Kumiko started to say, but then she shut her mouth. But Nukui knew what she wanted to say after that.

"I'm sorry."

"It's okay. It's me who should apologize," Nukui said. He knew he had to apologize now or lose the opportunity forever.

Nukui was certain that what his wife had been about to say was, *And then, my dad wanted to be able to hold our baby in his arms.*

Nukui's voice tightened, and he shed a tear.

"I…there was always something wrong with me. At first it was because I was so young, then I had to change jobs, but those were all made-up excuses."

"It's okay, Kyoichi. Stop."

"I…I was always afraid of becoming a father. The real reason is that simple. I could picture your belly getting bigger and bigger every day, and it just scared me so much. I couldn't stand it."

"Stop. Please."

"I never realized that having an abortion would be such a dangerous thing. It's my fault.

"I'm so sorry," Nukui said over and over, must have been

ten times, like a child. After that his words just trailed off.

His back was shaking. His wife laid her hand on it. It was so tender.

"Kyoichi, it's all right. I knew what I was doing. I knew why you were so upset about it. It was the only time you ever got so angry at me. Never before that, never since, just that once. I'm sorry. You don't have to cry anymore."

That night, Nukui and his wife slept in full embrace, like a pair of lovebirds.

She kissed him hard and clumsily, the way she did the first night, twenty years before.

·4·

Just like Tsunohazu, there were other old names for parts of Shinjuku that didn't appear on maps anymore: Yodobashi, Kashiwagi, Juniso.

"What could be more outrageous than having the name of your neighborhood, where you were born and raised, disappear, just for someone else's convenience," Yasuo said over drinks.

"Just think about, Kyoichi. All those rascals just buying up and selling our neighborhood where we grew up and then running off to the next place, and the city government just jabbers about it and does nothing."

This all sounded a little bit like sour grapes.

In this neighborhood, right next to the new city government center, land prices were said to have risen to a peak of one hundred million yen per *tsubo*. It was understandable that many people who had lived there all their lives took the opportunity to sell their ancestral properties.

It was also understandable that Yasuo, who had not taken that opportunity to sell his home, and who was now forced to pay enormous amounts of property tax and inheritance tax on top of that, was now feeling a bit remorseful.

Kyoichi and his wife had decided they wanted to spend their last day in Japan in the house they had grown up in, in Yodobashi. Kumiko and Yasuo's wife had taken the children and gone shopping. How many years had it been since Nukui had had a chance to sit and talk with Yasuo over a quiet drink?

"It's too bad Kumiko ended up never having any kids. I guess the two of you were just too close."

"Don't be silly. I was just always too busy."

The night before, before they fell asleep, Nukui and Kumiko had talked about finding a Japanese baby in Rio to adopt.

Now, Nukui was sitting looking at Yasuo's tiny garden in a soft afternoon rain. Just beyond the rotting wooden fence posts was a new concrete building, but by some kind of miracle this house was still standing.

"Nagashima is sixty this year, can you believe it? I can't believe it."

"You're kidding! I can't believe it either. We must be getting old too. I always felt a special connection to him because we had the same player number."

The afternoon alcohol had made Yasuo a little tipsy, and he was beaming.

In elementary school, Yasuo had played third base and batted fourth in the order. He had bequeathed his auspicious number to Kyoichi, the benchwarmer, and he never let anybody complain about it.

"They say the elementary school's going to be torn down."

"You're kidding!"

"That'll be a sad day. All three of us went there."

"Me from the second term of second grade."

"Kyoichi, you were always the best, from the day you got here. Isn't it amazing—I mean we're second cousins and all, but we're just different. Nobody could ever believe it."

"Did that put pressure on you?"

"No, that's not what I mean. I could see we were just different, right to the tips of our noses."

Yasuo and Kyoichi were the same age, but after middle school Yasuo had gone on to a technical high school and later inherited the family business. Kyoichi had gone to a municipal high school. For ten years Kyoichi and Yasuo had shared a four-and-a-half-mat room, sleeping in bunk beds, until Kyoichi was accepted at Tokyo University and went to live in the dormitory in Komaba.

He looked at the sliding paper door, smudged with handprints. Beyond the four-and-a-half-mat room they had shared was another three-mat room that had been Kumi-chan's. And this six-mat living room. No matter how hard the times, it can't have been easy to raise a family in this tiny house, let alone take in an extra child.

For example, and this was no more than vulgar speculation, Nukui believed his aunt and uncle had stopped doing the things that couples do when they were still in their mid-thirties.

Opening the glass front door, Nukui looked back at the workshop area. In the past, the place had been chockablock with old wooden buckets, but now it was neat and tidy, and the brand new buckets were neatly arranged.

"They were returned to the supermarket. I thought I'd sell them here, but nobody ever buys them. Cedar wood buckets, who needs them?" Yasuo remarked in lonely self-mockery. But then he added without missing a beat, as if he had just grasped what this conversation was really about, "Kyoichi, I've had something on my mind, and I haven't been able to bring it up until now. Do you mind?"

"What is it? No need to be so formal…"

Setting down his glass, Yasuo stretched seriously to his full height and said, "The house. I'm thinking of selling it."

Yasuo kneeled, with his tradesman's knuckles straight

and upright at his knees, in a formal posture of begging for understanding.

"We fell behind on the taxes, and now business is as you see. We should have sold when prices were better, but with this and that we never got around to it. Rather than have it seized and put up for auction, I'm thinking we'd be better off selling outright, even if we can't get a good price."

"If it's just a matter of money, we have some. Because we sold the condo."

"No, I couldn't do that," Yasuo said, waving his hands. "I appreciate your offering, but that wouldn't be right. We'll be okay for a little while, but not forever. We should just sell the house, liquidate everything we have, and buy a condo in the suburbs somewhere. That's what the bank says anyway."

"Yasuo, what will you do, where will you go?"

"One of my suppliers says I can work for them. At this point in my career it'll be strange to start working for hourly wages."

"Does Kumiko know about this?"

Yasuo paused a moment before replying and offered Kyoichi some more beer.

"I haven't told her. Since she married and moved out, it isn't her house anymore."

Kyoichi started to respond, but then he swallowed back his own words. Yasuo might have been blunt, but what he said was true.

"I would like to have your okay though. Do you think this would be disrespectful to my parents?"

When it came to disrespecting elders, Kyoichi was guilty as well. Busy with his work, he had never been able to repay his aunt and uncle for all they had done for him. And on top of that, he had made Kumiko unhappy.

"Kumiko told me a little bit about what's been going on with you. You're busy and I just went ahead and did it. I've made a mess of things."

The house was surrounded by the walls of bigger buildings, blocking the sunshine. The wind chime that had hung at the edge of the tiny garden since their childhood gave a lonesome ring.

What if Yasuo took the old nameplate reading "Kyoichi Nukui" and hung it outside his suburban condo too? Picturing this in his mind, Kyoichi felt as if his chest had been emptied out, and he hung his head. There were just too many things he had to say, but he only managed to say one: "Yasuo. I have made Kumiko unhappy."

Kyoichi had never been one to fool around. In twenty years, he may have gone out drinking once in a while, but his wife was the only woman he had ever been with. Even so, he believed, and regretted from the bottom of his heart, that he had made his wife unhappy.

"What are you talking about?" Yasuo asked, puzzled. "A trading company employee's wife knows that an overseas assignment goes with the territory."

Kyoichi's heart was screaming, *That's not what I mean.*

That night, on the street, the apparitions of his family members had come back to him one by one. His aunt's warm hands. Kumi-chan as a child, running up to him, clinging to him. His uncle, seldom speaking, but smiling from the narrow porch. Yasuo waving both hands in welcome.

His family members had reached a kindly decision. Their distant relative had come to them as a youth with a lump of unhappiness in his chest like a ball of steel. And at that time they had dared to wager everything they had to salve his pain.

Even after he finished at Tokyo University and got his job with the trading company, his uncle knew that Kyoichi's wounds were not fully healed. And that was why he sent Kumiko to him, with orders to continue treating Kyoichi's pain, forever.

And still Kyoichi thought to himself he had made her unhappy.

"What are you talking about, Kyoichi? Kumiko is happy."

No she isn't, Yasuo, Kyoichi thought. *That night, because of the pain I was suffering, I made her unhappy. I stole from her her birthright, to become a mother. This is what it comes down to.*

Kyoichi wondered if the day would ever come when he would be able to confess all of this to Yasuo.

The unexpected phone call came just as they were about to leave.

How did Oda know where he was? When Nukui asked him, Oda replied that because the telephone in Nukui's apartment was cut off, he had just looked up the old phone number in the employee directory.

The truth was, Oda had first called just about every hotel in Tokyo and the surrounding area, and then started asking all the employees in the office, trying to think of other places Nukui might be, before he thought to call his old family home. It had been quite a search, but he had finally guessed right.

And then, as if he knew all along that that's where Nukui would be, he said in a normal tone, "So glad I could reach you before you left. Which flight are you taking, the Varig Brasil at seven or the JAL at ten?"

"I thought I told you not to worry about that. If I tell you, what are you planning to do?"

"Please let me see you off. Just me."

"Cut it out. We're past having to make amends for that project. I'm taking all the blame and moving on to my next incarnation. You all will have to find your own paths to Buddha-hood. Now leave me alone."

Just as Nukui was about to hang up, Oda raised his voice and said, "There was an internal announcement today. As of September I'm to take your former position, as a special assignment."

"Is that so? Well, congratulations. It's an important post, and right in the spotlight. I'm sure you'll do well. I'm happy for you, Oda. My heart can rest easy now."

And then in a low voice, as if someone were strangling him, Oda said, "Do things like this really happen? They're letting me pass over you, as if nothing happened?"

"Hey, hey. Is anyone else there with you?"

"Yes, but I don't care. Just tell me the truth, Mr. Nukui. Things this stupid just don't really happen, do they? Okada is becoming head of the planning department, and Toyama head of the secretariat. You're the only one left out. Everyone else involved in that project is getting a promotion. We are all here, and we are all crying. Shall I pass the phone to someone else?"

"No, that's all right. It just means that all of you who worked for me are very talented. That's all."

"That's not it. There must be something else. You understand, don't you? We all...I'm sorry, I'm a little upset. We all trained under you. From the time we first entered the company until we had our first managerial positions, you're the one who mentored all of us."

"Oda, stop this. You are all very talented. I was lucky to have such talented people working for me."

Nukui could hear the voices of his agitated associates in the background. They must have been listening to the call on speakerphone.

"Now there's nothing left for us but revenge. We were all just talking about it. We don't care if we all get passed over for promotion, we just want you to be back here at the head office working with us."

"Stop saying such stupid things!" Nukui shouted. For a second there was silence on the other end of the line. "In ten years, when you're an executive, then we can talk about it. Okay? This is my final order to you. Don't waste your time thinking about small stuff. All of you—Oda, Toyama,

Okada—I want you all to become senior executives of the company. If you're all on the board of directors, then you can bring me back to the main office. I will pay no attention unless it is an order from the company itself, backed by a regular vote."

Oda was sobbing.

Ten years. Even if the three of them were able to carry out this order, little would be left of Nukui's career with the trading company once he came back from Rio.

"We have no excuse. We will do what we can." Oda said this, and his pledge was echoed by the others.

"There is no need to see me off. This is our honeymoon trip, and we don't need you," Nukui said and set down the receiver.

·5·

Rio. The backside of the earth. The farthest place in the world from Japan.

The flight from Narita to Rio would take twenty-one hours, with a layover in Los Angeles.

Nukui had spent a quarter-century circling the globe, but this was one branch he had never been to.

His predecessor in the post was an old man, more than a decade older than Nukui, and he had been left there in Rio like a forgotten sock at the laundromat. Nukui had called the man before the personnel department had reached him and told him he would be taking over. The man treated it like some kind of bad joke and told Nukui to knock it off.

Once Nukui's assignment was done he would be just about old enough to retire. Even if he returned to Japan there was nothing left he wanted to accomplish there, so he had gone through the procedures for permanent residency in Brazil. He planned to spend the rest of his days on a coffee plantation run by a Japanese-Brazilian. Not a bad life.

If the Japanese landscape passing the taxi window seemed like an old black-and-white movie, it must have been because of Nukui's hardening despondency. He felt nothing: not anger, not hope, not grief.

He was surprised that he was still feeling the afternoon beer he had drunk with Yasuo. His hands and feet were strangely warm and comfortable. He felt he was neither fully asleep nor fully awake, just hazily watching the Shinjuku scene go by.

It was evening rush hour, and the inbound highway on-ramp near the new city center was closed. They still had time before their ten o'clock flight. Nukui asked the taxi driver to go back to Yasukuni-dori and get on the highway from the old city center ramp.

"Kumiko, can I ask something a little odd?"

"Sure. It's nothing shocking, is it?" she answered him, as they stared sadly out at their old neighborhood.

"Do you remember my father?"

"Sort of. He wore glasses, right? He always wore a necktie and a suit. And he smelled of pomade."

"He was sort of a dandy. I must admit that's an accurate description. And he always wore a hat."

The headquarters building of Nukui's company was obscured by rainclouds from the middle up.

"Remember there used to be a water treatment plant right here? We used to fish here."

"The security man used to chase us, didn't he, Kumiko? And once he caught you."

"Yes. My brother ran off, but you came back to help me. I think that's when I started liking you, a little."

"I went back, but it wasn't just to help you."

"Is that so? I'm disappointed."

"I just didn't want to be a coward. I never wanted to be a coward."

His intention had been to express some pride in his life, but this was not something he could turn to his wife and say.

A soft rain continued to fall over Shinjuku. At dusk they reached the big guardrail that stood over Kabuki-cho, and finally his wife responded to him, as if she just remembered something.

"Kyoichi, I've been thinking about yesterday."

Kyoichi didn't answer but looked out at the sea of umbrellas going this way and that.

"It was a hallucination. If you keep obsessing about things like that, you'll go crazy. They say dementia begins at forty. I heard it on TV."

A hallucination. He did not believe in ghosts or spirits or time travel. There was just one thing he wanted to believe in.

He wanted to believe that after he had boarded that last bus and gone to his uncle's house, his father had broken up with that woman and come back to Tsunohazu to meet him. And that he had then run around the streets till dawn, asking every passerby and bum and shopkeeper whether they had seen a boy about eight years old.

And when he got tired of searching, if he had gone back to that woman, that would be okay. Even if he still wanted to abandon his child, that would be okay. Nukui just wanted to believe that his father had come back to look for him, even if it was only to tell him that he was leaving him. Of course there were circumstances. Even he himself had killed his own child for his own selfish reasons, so he could not attack his father. But he wished he had been more of a man and not lied about it, just left him and been done with it.

The taxi was driving down the big main avenue of Shinjuku, where the neon lights were just coming on. Kyoichi focused intently on the mob at the bus stop, looking for his father.

More than anything, he wanted to see him again. For the sake of his wife, who was now accompanying him to an unknown place into a life in banishment through no fault of her own, he wanted to put everything back together again. The taxi was passing through the bustle of Tsunohazu.

Exhaling and sinking deep into his seat, Kyoichi peered deep down the path to Hanazono Shrine, where he thought he saw someone in a white summer suit.

"Sorry, but could you stop here for a minute?"

The car came to a sudden stop just before the traffic light. "What's wrong?"

"Nothing, nothing important. I just thought I'd pop into Hanazono Shrine and get a fortune for our trip. I'll be right back. Just wait here a sec."

In all likelihood it had just been another illusion. The path ahead was obscured by mist.

A stand of gingko and cherry trees lined the approach to Hanazono Shrine. Before passing under the *torii* arch, Nukui straightened his necktie and buttoned his suit jacket.

"Dad...?"

Under the overhanging trees, the paving stones were dark, but in a circle of light from a streetlamp Nukui saw his father standing, quite relaxed. Hemp summer suit, Panama hat. Same as the last time he had seen him.

"Ah, Kyoichi, I've been looking for you. Is this where you've been?"

The lights of Yasukuni-dori were reflected in his eyeglasses.

"You came back for me..."

His father hesitated, then slowly took a step toward Kyoichi, whose nose filled with the familiar scent of his father's pomade.

What in the world did they have to talk about?

"Did you see, Dad? Nagashima did join the Giants after all."

"Is that so? Say, you and I never had a chance to play catch."

"That's okay. I've been playing with Yasuo every day. And uncle bought me a uniform. My number is 3."

As he listened, Nukui's father hung his head. He was silent for a moment, and then pushed his glasses up his nose and said, "There's something I need to talk to you about. Do you have a minute?"

"Sure. What is it? I promise not to cry or get angry. I just want to know what you're thinking. Tell me everything."

He approached his father close enough to reach out and touch him. His father nodded. The two men were exactly the same height.

"Things with your dad are terrible right now."

"Yeah. I know."

"Your mom died, the company went bust. I just can't hang around Tokyo anymore. I have to go somewhere far away, but there's no way I can go there with a little boy. And on top of that, that woman, she says if you go with me she won't go."

It was as if his father had put his child and his woman on a balance-scale. Actually, no, it was different. Without a doubt, he had chosen this path as a way of ensuring his child's happiness. The expression on his face was full of pain, but his eyes were kind.

And then his father said, "Kyoichi. I'm sorry to say this, but I have to leave you here."

This was the one thing Kyoichi needed to hear. He tugged on the sleeve of his suit jacket and held it to his eyes and cried.

His father's hand touched him on the shoulder. Sobbing audibly, for the first time in his life Kyoichi boasted. "Dad, I, I became a salaryman just like you said. I studied hard, and I went to college, and I became a salaryman just like you always wanted to be."

His father looked closely at Kyoichi's appearance.

"Is that so? Well, that's terrific. You've really made

something of yourself."

"No one was better than me. Not in elementary school, not in middle school, not in high school. I was always number one. No one was ever better than me. Even after I joined this company, I was always number one."

"You always tried really hard, Kyoichi."

"Yes, I did. But to tell the truth, I was never all that smart, because I was your son."

"Hey, hey, that was mean."

"And on top of that, I'm timid and weak. So I had to try that much harder. So that's why, right? I mean, orphans have to try harder to stay ahead. 'Cause if they lose, everybody says it's just because they're orphans, 'cause their father left them. That's what people say. But that puts the blame on the mom and dad, and that's just impossible. I mean, that kind of talk is what the number two guy always has to put up with from the number one guy, so I could never let myself be beaten by anyone."

As he listened, Nukui's father pursed his lips as if to contain his welling emotions. He pushed back the brim of his Panama hat and looked up at the streetlamp.

The truth was even harsher. In the end, he started to say, he had become an outstanding salaryman, but he had never become a father, but then he bit his lip. He had no wish to make his father suffer.

In some cooler corner of his brain, he realized this was merely the ghost of his father. And if that were the case, his father was no longer of this world. The joy of seeing his father again suddenly gave way to deep sadness.

"Dad."

"What is it?"

"Are you dead?"

Instead of answering, his father hid his face behind his hat. His lips were trembling.

"Where did you die? When? How?"

For a dead person, that was the toughest question in the world. Nukui's father had to take several deep breaths against the pain.

"I died in Kyushu. Not long after I left you. My liver was shot. Alcohol and drugs."

"So that's why you never came back to get me."

His head was still bowed. Tears dripped from Nukui's father's narrow jaw.

"I did call, from the hospital. More than anything, I wanted to see you again before I died."

"I never heard anything about that."

"Your uncle probably never told you. He thought it would be too much for you, to see me. He chided me. But he did do the one thing I asked him to do, I think."

"What did you ask him to do?"

The wind blew through the tree branches. Big tears fell noisily on Nukui's father's Panama hat. Silently, his father raised his head.

"I told him I would definitely be back for you, so I asked him never to change your name. It would never do to change your name. That would be pitiful."

"That was just selfish of you. I wanted to be their child."

"I knew already I would never be able to go back to Tokyo to see you again. My body couldn't take it. But I didn't want you to become someone else's child. We had lived together so long, just the two of us."

Deep in his mind, Kyoichi remembered the lonely life the two of them had led after his mother died. For two years his father had been both father and mother to him.

"Forgive me, Dad. I think I finally understand. You were tired. That's it, isn't it? Your company went bust, and you had to cook every day and do the laundry. You must have reached the end of your rope. Forgive me. I never understood."

"None of that is any reason for me to abandon my child.

I just wasn't made for bringing up a kid. I was a coward. I destroyed my body, and I never showed up to get you. That's why there was one more favor I asked of your uncle."

"What was that?"

For the first time, Nukui's father smiled.

"You know what it was, don't you?"

"...No, I don't. What did you ask him?"

"I asked him, even if I was never able to come get you, never to leave you alone. You always were a lonesome sort. I asked him to let Kumiko marry you, so you would always be related. And he did, right?"

Kyoichi looked his father straight in the eye, and he nodded. As only a parent could, before he left his father had provided for him a secure future.

"Is everything going okay?"

In all probability, the only woman in the world who could understand him for himself, who could have made him happy, was Kumiko.

Still smiling, the figure of Kyoichi's father faded into the mist. Kyoichi stood at attention and bowed his head deeply.

"Thank you, Dad. Thank you so much."

His father's voice could still be heard. "I'm sorry for all the trouble I caused you. Forgive me, Kyoichi."

When Kyoichi lifted his head, all he could see was the darkened trees, wet with rain.

His wife stood behind him, holding an umbrella over his head.

"What about the paper fortune?"

"Ah, the fortune. The shrine office was already closed. Let's get going."

"You're a strange one, you are. Visiting a shrine at this hour."

Passing back under the *torii* arch, Kyoichi looked back at the wet paving stones.

"Kumiko..."

"What is it, dear? What is it? What did you say?"

"Kumiko. Have I made a mess of things?"

"Never mind. It doesn't matter. It's still a little embarrassing to hear you call me that."

Tsunohazu was in a haze of rain. Nukui doubted his father would ever appear on these streets again.

Under the umbrella, he put his arm around his wife's shoulders. It occurred to him that once they arrived at Narita Airport, they might have time before their flight to eat some sushi. He would be able to leave his home with no unfinished business, no lingering attachments.

Kyara

I wasn't sure exactly where the shop was.

I remembered it as being near Prince Hitachi's palace in Hiroo, probably because that was how the friend who told me about it described it to me.

I looked for it a few years ago, out of a sense of nostalgia, but the neighborhood had changed so completely there were practically no clues to connect the present with the past.

It had been more than twenty years. Most likely it had all been buried beneath the new road that ran across the Shibuya bridge from Ebisu to Tameike-dori.

Because it was so near the prince's palace, more than likely this had been one of Tokyo's most exclusive neighborhoods of expensive estates in the days before the forests of condominiums had gone up. Even when I tried to remember, it was a bit strange to think that such a charming little boutique had stood in such a place.

But there was no mistake about it—that was where the shop had been, hidden on a steeply sloping street with loose cobblestones between the walls of the old estates, where the massive trunks of zelkova and ginkgo trees spread their branches against the sky.

Using a vague map scrawled on a bar napkin, I got close to the place, but gave up, turned the wheel, and headed back.

It was a hot, sticky night, and a light rain was falling. The

JIRO ASADA

windshield wipers were working, and suddenly the glare of a reflective sign struck my eyes. More than feeling relief at having finally found it, I remember being surprised by it. As if to aggravate my irritation, it had simply suddenly appeared, on a spot of road I had already passed several times.

No, that wasn't right. This steep stretch of road lined with ginkgo trees, a white guardrail running along one side, was so typical of Tokyo's elegant neighborhoods that if the appearance of the shop seemed to be sudden, it must have been an illusion on my part. On this signless one-lane street, enfolded deep in the mist—I must have just overlooked it.

The name of the shop was Kyara.

No matter what onerous quota looms, no matter what money problems or woman problems he has, a salesman has to be sunny when he's dealing with customers. The truth is that's the only thing we really have to do. For salesmen working in the fashion industry, and having to deal with the sometimes tough businesswomen who run these small boutiques, having good taste is just part of the job.

The kinds of guys who become top salesmen for any kind of clothing company are as a rule neither particularly handsome nor particularly fashionable themselves. We tend to be likable types who are good at flattery and clowning around. The only time we ever put on a suit and tie, it's either to call on customers at New Year's or when we're invited to some customer's show in a hotel banquet room. Most of the time, for routine sales calls, we generally dress more casually.

On that particular day, I was wearing a red checked shirt and white jeans. My predecessor in this sales territory had warned me, however, that while older shop proprietresses may like casual and even cute, they would never put up with someone who was less than meticulous about his appearance.

For this reason, my working "uniform" always included white jeans that were absolutely wrinkle-free. I can recall what shirt I was wearing that day because I remember that, before entering the shop, I carefully inspected my reflection in the show window. Kyara was the kind of boutique you could tell at a glance was top-drawer.

For a prêt-a-porter shop, location is not the most important factor determining sales. No matter how out of the way, a store with a loyal customer base exudes a certain ambiance, even from the outside.

I was beginning to understand why this sales colleague, who owed me a thing or two, would take me aside to give me a special tip about this place.

Maybe because it stood so deep in the trees, I can't remember now whether the shop was in a house or whether it was a rented portion of a bigger building. My recollection is that it was the first floor of an old maisonette in that neighborhood of antique estates.

The outside walls were covered with ivy. The window boxes in front of the show window were planted with impatiens, and to the side was a tree with pale pink flowers. It was only much later that I learned that tree was called a crape myrtle.

In my experience, crape myrtle flowers are generally fierce-looking, suggesting oppressive heat. But the crape myrtles planted next to Kyara seemed to be a different sort, somehow more refined, more tranquil: the glossy trunk, the leaves, the pale pink flowers.

The entrance to the shop was a bit lower than the pavement and laid with lapis-colored tiles. There was a white luminescent sign that did not quite fit the exterior look, but beside the big door with the brass handle there was a coppery green lamp that was a fine piece of workmanship.

At first glance the boutique did not appear to be the sort of place that sold ready-to-wear. Judging by both its looks and its location, it would be easy to think it dealt in old-fashioned, custom-made haute couture.

After checking my appearance in the show window, I opened the door and entered with the customary greeting in my company-issued salesman's voice.

From behind the velvet curtains in the back, a woman's voice answered, "I'll be right with you."

"Mr. Kotani from Boulogne suggested I stop by. Sorry to come so late in the day."

Again the woman said faintly, "I'll be right with you," but no one emerged from behind the curtains. I thought she must have been arranging her hair. I could smell perfume.

The room was square and measured about ten *tsubo*. While waiting for the woman to come out, I had a look around the shop and inspected the wares hanging on the racks.

She had good taste. All the clothes were from well-known, high-quality manufacturers, and gave the impression of having been chosen by a knowing eye. It was mid-August, but not a single garment had short sleeves. All were new items for fall, a testament to the competence of the management.

If looking back now it seemed the light was a bit dim, it may be because my memory is growing old. There's no reason for a boutique to be dark inside.

As I was gazing at an antique tapestry hanging on the wall, the shop proprietress finally emerged from behind the velvet curtain.

"Hello…"

For an instant I was completely taken aback by the woman's beauty, and I lost the thread of what I was saying.

Whether attractive or ugly, boutique owners are invariably of a type that is never missing from old-fashioned samurai sword-fighter stories: poisonous middle-aged women. Accustomed as I was to doing business with such women, the graceful impression this one made of a young wife from one of the nearby estates was quite unexpected.

"Mr. Kotani from Boulogne suggested I stop by."

She accepted my business card, and I noticed that her

hands were as white as porcelain.

"Ah, yes. Mr. Kotani called me. I see you represent a top manufacturer, San Dominico of Minami-Aoyama."

Without a trace of pretentiousness, the woman spoke in an old-fashioned Tokyo dialect that I thought had vanished long ago. It sounded not in the least unnatural.

Her jet-black hair was bound in an elegant chignon. Judging by the sounds I had just heard from beyond the curtain as she combed her hair, it was very long.

"I am quite familiar with your company's products. Would the same terms as Boulogne's be all right?"

She smiled, causing very attractive little wrinkles to form at the corners of her eyes. I guessed she was in her mid-thirties.

From the way she so abruptly brought up the business terms I could sense her backbone, and I responded with my own natural affability.

"That's a lovely dress you're wearing. Is it silk?"

Her dress was charcoal gray and had a big pleat at the bust. No one wore long silk satin dresses in those days. It was midsummer. I was pretty sure it was rayon or polyester, but praising your customer's taste was a tried-and-true technique in fashion sales.

"Thank you for the compliment. But it's synthetic."

As if she were dancing the minuet, she raised the hem of her dress and faced me. The material had lightness and softness and that unmistakable sheen that made me certain it was in fact very fine silk satin.

I'm pretty sure she was tall. Or maybe she simply had a way of stretching her spine and her long neck that gave the appearance of height.

She opened the old-fashioned cash register and presented to me her name card, in a fancy font on Japanese paper.

Boutique Kyara
Shizuka Tachibana

"Seems almost like a stage name."

"I don't really care for the word 'boutique,' and it's just the name of the store, but still it somehow makes it seem like a bar."

I turned toward the window, smiling, unable to look straight at her small, oval face.

The crape myrtle tree was wet from the rain. Two mannequins in elegant dresses were reflected in the glass, as if they were standing outside on the dark, sloping street.

I couldn't see the reflection of the woman, but I attributed that to the light or the angle. Perhaps, right after her initial pleasantries, she had gone off to make tea or something like that.

We drank tea scented with roses, sitting in amber-colored rattan chairs on either side of a table. I have no recollection at all of my conversation with Shizuka Tachibana after that.

It's hard to explain exactly why things were going so well for the fashion industry at that time.

It was a time when there was plenty of money in the world, and people suddenly felt they needed to be fashionable every day. Until that time, women's wear had basically come in two categories: everyday clothing and haute couture. Into the gap between them came a completely new fashion concept: prêt-a-porter.

Who was it who had decided to use the word *boutique* to describe stores that dealt exclusively in this particular kind of merchandise, that were not really just an accessories shop, not really just a clothing shop?

For women liberated from housework or who had entered the working world, prêt-a-porter clothing became as essential to life as business suits were for men. Manufacturers heeding these demands of the times showed tremendous growth, and the boutique retailers that supplied the goods were popping up all over Tokyo.

The way this all happened was revolutionary. The fashion industry grew by leaps and bounds, but those of us on the working end of things were forever being tossed about by seasons and trends, working morning, noon, and night.

I would always arrive at the office early, write my sales reports for the day before, and look over my new samples. I would pack the van full of suits and dresses and head out for that day's boutiques. Salesmen are responsible for everything from developing routes to routine consultations to making deliveries and collecting payments. If you're going to meet your quotas, you can't afford to pay any attention to some calendar showing days on and days off. All of us at this end of the business are chronically fatigued.

There were a few favored resting places for urban salesmen along the main streets of Aoyama and Azabu. Deep in the night, when the day's work was done, we would gather our vans of various colors by the side of the road somewhere, belly up to the counter of some chichi bar, grumble a little, joke a little, and let slip a little bit of precious information.

The place where Kotani from Boulogne had told me about his good customer was a shot bar in Nishi-Azabu decorated with blue neon lights.

"Listen here. Swear you'll never tell anyone else. No one."

He had made it all sound so ridiculously important.

"With such a lousy location it sounds like the sort of place no other salesman would ever just stumble upon, even by mistake. Evening dresses for early summer, and plenty of them. And she pays in cash, no discounts, no returns."

Hmm, I thought to myself, laughing through my nose. This kind of "good customer" Kotani was telling me about had caused me plenty of pain in the past.

"Sounds to me like Koen-ji, part two. No discounts, no returns? You said the same thing back then."

"Nah, this is different. I'm telling you about this to make up for that. But I see. Never mind. From what I've seen that shop has room for goods from just about one more supplier. I thought maybe you'd like to try it."

Boulogne and San Dominico were direct competitors. The key concept of the two companies was the same, aimed at career women as their main customer, and they used a lot of the same fabrics and the same factories. The two companies were such close rivals the chief designer had moved from one to the other just the year before.

If the two of us had not been the top salesmen in our respective companies, we might have been true friends.

"If this place is such a good customer, why are you telling me about it? If San Dominico products make any real headway there, it'll just be a problem for you."

"Not at all," Kotani said, standing up the collar of his polo shirt. "I just think we should be fair about things like that. The way I look at it, I would rather it be just us, instead of having some company I don't know anything about come barging in there."

"So you're thinking about making it into an exclusive shop for Boulogne and San Dominico...That wouldn't be so bad."

I thought this was sweet. That was about the time when our sales were hitting a ceiling, with the economy starting to slow down and an excess supply of product. A shop that would pay 100 percent up front, in cash, with no discounts and no returns, you knew what must have been going on. The owner was some kind of amateur: the wife, or maybe the mistress, of some gazillionaire.

Kotani appeared to be reading my thoughts as he lifted the corner of his mouth in a smile over the lip of his glass.

And that's the quick summary of how I came to know about Kyara.

The first time I ever visited there, on that rainy evening, I sold thirty fall suits. Top-season goods, at my asking price. That took care of several days' work in just one hour.

If I wanted to try harder, everything I brought in and recommended, Shizuka Tachibana would have bought. But I couldn't do that. The conventional wisdom of selling to amateur boutique operators was that they should be handled slowly, kept in a state somewhere between life and death.

I didn't go back to Kyara again until autumn. I figured about the time the fall collections were all out on the sales floor and it was time to collect some money, that would be a good time to really get down to business.

Given that sooner or later any business run as a hobby is bound to go under, the true test of a good salesman is the ability to know just exactly how long he can expect to milk a living out of it.

Kotani hadn't said that so plainly, but I bet in the back of his mind he was thinking the same thing.

·2·

Early in September, my boss came back from a long business trip.

He said he had been buying some fabrics and doing some market research, but I knew it had been a pleasure trip overseas. It was already the time when good suit fabric from Europe was no longer hard to get. The most important thing was to have an ex-model as a self-styled designer. There was no such thing as market research.

But talk like that was taboo at the company. The boss had achieved great success just five years after going independent, and his unique appearance and outrageous behavior were just part of the Aoyama San Dominico brand.

Over the radio in the inspection office, I heard that a big typhoon was approaching.

Outside, a warm damp wind was swirling. A blue Porsche came slithering down the underground ramp. The boss emerged wearing a jacket that matched the color of the car. He tossed the keys to the rather agitated section chief who had come out to greet him and started complaining indiscriminately.

"This car needs washing. Who packed so much product into it? Why is the office so messy?" All of this was just his typical morning greeting.

I was there unloading a bunch of freshly pressed items from the aluminum van, and he fixed me in his gaze and called my name. My car was always shiny as a button, but in his absence I had been loafing, as usual. Of course, there was nothing that would warrant a formal reprimand.

"I want to see you in my office right away," he said, a puzzled look on his face.

"Welcome back, boss. I hope you had a good trip."

He made not the least effort at a response and boarded the elevator.

Ours was a new company, but it had sixty employees, and it was rare indeed for a rank-and-file salesman to set foot in the president's office. The gaudy decor reflected the boss's taste for the ostentatious, and I sat stiffly on the sofa and waited for whatever I had coming to me.

The boss sent the secretary away and read through some documents as he toyed with the gold chain at his open collar.

"I hear you did ten million yen's worth of business in August. Pretty impressive."

With one elbow on his desk he glanced sidelong in my direction. They say a man's allure can be measured by the number of women he's had, and it seemed to be the truth.

Whenever I encountered that kind of unfakeable allure, I always envied men at forty.

He had not called me here to chew me out. In just an instant, he returned to his usual unpleasant expression, got up from his desk, and sat down again across from me.

"Listen to me. You've got to get rid of those white jeans. They make you look like a kid."

No way he called me in here to tell me that.

"I could look all over Tokyo for a salesman who can sell ten million yen in midsummer and never find one. Those guys all wear white shirts and ties."

The boss took out a slim cigar for himself and offered one to me. There was a bay window at shoulder height, and it was filled with autumn color, like a silk screen.

"When you were working the outside as a salesman, did you used to wear a white shirt and necktie?" I asked, simply. I wasn't trying to talk back to him. I just couldn't picture him dressed like that.

Blowing a plume of smoke from his thin lips, the boss smiled a strained smile.

"No. I wore white jeans."

Placing the two fingers that still gripped his cigar to his temple, he thought for a minute. That the jacket draped over his shoulders appeared to fade into the autumn sky framed by the bay window must have been just a trick of the mind.

Again he looked straight at me and said, "I want you to tell me more about your customer in Hiroo."

"Which Hiroo customer do you mean?"

"The new one, where you delivered goods."

"Oh, you mean Kyara."

When I said the name, the boss shut his eyes hard, as if remembering some past pain.

So I rattled off a few facts as they came into my head, that Kotani from Boulogne had told me about it, that it was in an out-of-the-way location but seemed to have loyal customers, and that I had dropped off thirty suits just to see how things would go.

"A new customer and you let them have thirty suits? You think that'll be okay?"

"We'll see how things go when I go to collect the first payment."

"That goes without saying. But I think maybe before that you should pay a visit, and if things aren't looking good you should pull the goods."

"Huh? You mean take them back?"

This was a strange directive. The boss generally hated weakness in salesmen.

"Do as I say. I know what you're thinking. In our business, you have to be choosy about your customers. Don't mess with that place."

Mess with was considered almost a technical term in our trade, and not one an executive in our industry used lightly about a customer.

A pattern cutter came into the office with a sample coat for the boss to examine, and I got up to leave, no wiser than I had been before. As I was closing the door, the boss called after me, "About that customer, you can let Boulogne have them. Don't bite off more than you can chew."

My boss's words were beyond my comprehension.

On my second visit to Kyara, that's right, instead of the crape myrtle that had lost its color, at its roots bloomed an amaryllis so red it seemed to be burning. It must have been mid-September.

It was late afternoon, the time of day when the people coming and going outside the show window cast unnaturally long shadows down the sloping street.

I commented on the beautiful flowers, at which Shizuka Tachibana squinted in the cutest way and said, "It's a strange flower, don't you think? It blooms in autumn, right around the equinox, as if it knows what day it is. I almost feel I should make an offering to it."

That day too she was wearing a silk satin dress with a big pleat at the bust. Her hair was again done up in a chignon, and I found her profile fascinating.

It was the first time I had ever been smitten by an older woman.

"Your dresses have been selling well. I think they're just about all gone."

As I sipped my rose-scented tea, I looked casually around the shop. On one rack that looked a bit sparse, I noticed a lot of clothes with Boulogne's distinctive silver tags.

"You seem to have added some Boulogne merchandise."

"That's because you never come around."

Through the show window came the red-orange light of the setting sun. Shizuka Tachibana crossed her legs and draped the hem of her long dress over the rattan chair.

"I hope you can leave some new clothes today. I am really beginning to like the San Dominico line."

Speaking in a voice so languorous it was hard to believe this was a business discussion, Shizuka Tachibana placed her finger against her slightly tilted cheek and smiled a faint smile. Her skin glowed in the evening light, and at twilight it was tinged with the colors of the dusk.

The sound of a time-weary cello flowed solemnly through the air.

"Might I ask a slightly strange question?"

"Of course. What is it?"

"I was wondering why you never wear any accessories. No necklace, no earrings."

As if she were being told this for the very first time, Shizuka Tachibana touched the neckline of her dress, near the fold, and then looked at her fingers, which were adorned by not a single ring.

"My work is to sell clothes. It would be rude to my

customers."

She saw her role as a stagehand, a prompter. But even in that sense, her beauty itself would be a problem. By declining to adorn her own body, she actually accentuated its beauty. Without a doubt, her customers would see her as arrogant and themselves as jealous.

"I am just a mannequin here."

The word gave me goose bumps. I was sure she merely meant to refer to herself as a saleswoman, but without thinking I found myself looking at the mannequins in the show window.

From her enamel handbag, Shizuka Tachibana pulled a fat envelope and laid it on the table.

"This payment isn't due quite yet, but why don't you take it? And if it's all right with you, I'd like you to leave some new clothes in exchange."

"You misunderstand me. That isn't what I was talking about."

"I'm sure your company must be giving you a little bit of a hard time about me. They're saying I bought too much for my first purchase. But as you can see, I've sold nearly all of it. And I didn't have to go to too much trouble to do it."

The envelope contained the full amount of the invoice. Kotani had been telling the truth.

"All for me?"

"Yes," she said, staring at me strangely. Her eyes were big and round, and lovely. That kind of easy money, offered with such naïveté, no salesman in the world could have done anything but smile and accept it.

"Is anything wrong?" she asked, looking straight at me.

Something was wrong. I was thinking about the trade argot, "mess with," and how ugly it was. Unable to look into the purity of her eyes, I turned away. And at that moment, before I could stop myself, the words sprang from my throat: "The customary practice is to pay 70 percent."

"Seventy percent?"

"Yes, that's just the way we usually do business. In case one of the dresses has a flaw or in case you have to return something. And then we just settle the differences at the end of the payment month. And usually that gets taken care of with an end-of-season discount, or something like that."

She thought for a while, as if she was trying to absorb what I had said.

"You mean, you're saying I only have to pay 70 percent, and that will take care of things?"

"That's right. That's all you have to pay."

"Nobody ever told me that before. What does this mean? I don't understand."

I felt almost as if I had just declared my love for her. Any other time I had ever decided to "mess with" some amateur shop owner, I had always done so with the cooperation of my pals. As far as sales were concerned, there probably wasn't any other salesman, even from the big companies, who could claim better numbers than me. The rumor about me was that anywhere my car left tire tracks, no weeds could grow.

"That's just the usual practice in this business. The profit margins in prêt-a-porter are good enough to support that."

"So does that mean that until now I've been paying 30 percent too much? To every company I've bought from?"

"No, that's not what I'm saying…" I wasn't sure how I should finish that sentence. In fact she had been paying 30 percent too much. The truth was, amateurs with money had been opening boutiques like mushrooms springing up after a rainstorm, and those of us who were salesman working for big manufacturers had been eating their lunch and getting fat on it. That was what we meant when we said we were going to "mess with" somebody.

"I wish I had never heard that…"

She folded her unadorned hands in her lap and sighed a small sigh.

That day, I took away just 70 percent of the invoiced amount and left her with a choice selection of the goods I had in my car. For the few dresses she hadn't been able to sell, I cut her a return slip and took them away.

"Well, if you treat me this way, won't you be in trouble?" she said, standing by the window of my car in the light of the setting sun.

"This is the way we treat all of our best old customers."

I will never forget her smile in the last light of the day.

As soon as I drove away, I wondered what had made me do that. People said apparel salesmen would steal the eyes from a live horse, and I myself had long since forgotten all about morality or virtue, but I never really was that type.

Maybe I was falling in love.

I couldn't think of a single reason why that would be.

·3·

One night at the end of the month, I saw Kotani at the shot bar in Nishi-Azabu.

"Looks like you're not doing too bad. Been out collecting on your invoices?"

Kotani came closer, putting a heavy-looking bag on the counter. He always was a clever man, and that night he was in a particularly good mood.

"You remember that shop? How much you think I made from there this month?"

"I wonder."

Kotani had put a friendly arm around my shoulder, but I turned my face away. For him to say something like that his sales must have been pretty good.

"One point eight mil. Can you believe it? As much as the main order for a chain store."

It was an unbelievable sum for a small boutique run by an individual. Sipping at his glass, Kotani smiled a cruel smile.

"Don't you think you might be overdoing it? I don't see how a store like that could afford that kind of money. I've never seen any customers there."

"You're wrong. Sales are good. She does have to sell on credit, though. The rich ladies in the big mansions and the fancy condominiums like to buy her stuff in quantity."

That explained it. If she was willing to sell like that, her customers would buy as much as they liked of anything that looked new. But that meant the more she sold, the bigger her own debts. How many stores had I known that had failed in the past by drowning in accounts receivable, selling to customers and letting them pay when they had the money?

"Say..." Kotani started to say, so close I could smell the alcohol on his breath. "I think you should put a little more of your heart in this. Don't make me the only bad guy here. If Boulogne is the only company taking advantage of her, it'll be too obvious, and when she gets into trouble it'll be like I drew you a picture and told you how to swindle her."

"I'm sure that's all true. And if a number of companies are involved, it'll be clear to everyone that the problem was on the buyer's side. Let her buy as much as she wants, and when she gets backed up she can write an IOU. Or we can introduce her to some sleazy moneylender, but at some point we'll have to play bank and cut back her inventory."

For an instant Kotani looked wounded, but before long he was beaming again and pounding me on the shoulder.

"What are you talking about? This is where you get to be the star. Or is it that you just don't like it that I was the one who gave you the tip to begin with? It's all just business, only business. I have a feeling this winter season, she's going to run out of cash. A small shop might get by for a year on IOUs, but bigger companies don't care about a few scars, and we'll cut her off. It's obvious."

From somewhere to the side of the counter, a young salesman from Palm Tree showed his face. Palm Tree was a new prêt-a-porter company that had split off from Boulogne about a year before.

"What do you mean, 'just business,' Kotani? Cut me in on this."

Kotani laughed through his nose.

"You guys, it's about ten years too soon for you to step inside the Yamanote Line."

"Introduce me to your customer, won't you? I won't make a mess of things. No matter how you slice it, our place in the world is right where Boulogne and San Dominico go head to head. We have trouble doing business there."

"You should head for the countryside, young man, the countryside. Somewhere out past Sendai, that's where you'll find people who will appreciate your crappy Palm Tree suits. Somewhere out on the Tohoku Highway."

"Gimme a break, Kotani. People out there don't understand anything about prêt-a-porter suits."

"They'll sell. Anywhere they have An-An and Non-No."

"That may be true for casual clothes, but career clothes like ours are a different story."

Kotani spat out his drink.

"Did you hear that? He said Palm Tree sells career clothes! All you guys ever do is take apart our products and San Dominico's and make copies. You dare to call that prêt-a-porter career clothes? Listen, before you start asking people favors, at least go out and hire a decent designer," Kotani said with a straight face. The Palm Tree salesman hung his head and started to slink away, but as he left he dropped his last remark, ever so quietly: "Kotani, do you believe women are witches?"

"Just what is that supposed to mean?"

"You shouldn't go around saying things that some woman might resent. Bad things could happen. It can get pretty scary."

On a street lined with platanus trees, there was a line of

parked vans of many colors. It was the end of the month, the salesmen were done with the rough part of their work, and they were thronging into the bar. The guy from Palm Tree mingled with the crowd and settled into a booth.

Kotani clucked his tongue and gulped his drink.

"Witches! What the hell does he think he's talking about?"

For a minute, all kinds of horrible thoughts flashed through my head. I didn't care what kind of picture he had drawn, 1.8 million yen in one month was just not normal.

"Say, you don't have something special going on with that lady at Kyara, do you?"

Kotani held his breath, his glass still held to his lips.

"And what if I did? You're a fine one to talk. You're the one who's taking the star turn here. Like we did at Koen-ji, like brothers. I've got no problems with whatever happens here."

I got up from my stool without a word.

I got into the car and drove away recklessly. Before returning to the office I decided I should hang out among the ginkgo trees in Gaien Park for a little while and sober up. I lay down on a bench and looked up at the leaves turning colors. All of a sudden I felt old at twenty-six. I felt like a juvenile delinquent coming to a decision that I couldn't live this way anymore. Above the art museum, a red full moon was rising.

·4·

I showed my face at Kyara once or twice a month.

I always went around the store's eight o'clock closing time. I had no interest in butting heads with Kotani. And neither did I want to see him together with Shizuka Tachibana.

After that, all the time, whether I was driving or working, or even when I was making love with a woman, the only thing I could think of was Shizuka Tachibana.

For all that, I knew absolutely nothing about her private life. Was she single? Did she have a family? Did she have a special patron? I made no attempt at knowing. On the contrary, I was afraid to know.

On my visits to Kyara, I never discussed anything but business. On top of that, I dropped off the winter items, which are generally more expensive, based just on provisional requests.

In front of the store, once the amaryllis had faded, impatiens bloomed. When those were done, there were cyclamens. All of these flowers blossomed as red as fantasy flames, but they were placid flowers.

Every time I stopped by, I noticed more Boulogne products. By the end of autumn, the place was looking like an exclusively Boulogne shop, the racks full of those distinctive, silvery aluminum tags.

It seemed things were progressing exactly according to the picture Kotani had painted: pile on the clothes and be tough about the money. Customers who are worried about payments are always pushing to sell more, so they are willing to buy more. Any time Kotani saw empty space on a rack, he found a way to fill it.

It was only too obvious where all this was heading. He would make her open a special bank account and write him an IOU. Once the IOUs were no good, he would send around the sleazy moneylenders.

Although I could see all this, I couldn't bring myself to do anything about it. There were other stores where I was up to the same tricks, so I was in no position to complain about Kotani's methods. It was another unwritten rule of our trade that we did not criticize another's business practices.

The Boulogne line was fantastic. At least at that time, Boulogne was the only other company in a position to cross swords with my own San Dominico in the career women's and the young women's markets. Once Boulogne clothes took over a certain portion of a sales area, all the other companies might as well give up.

I had no idea what Kotani had done to entice Shizuka Tachibana, nor did I want to know.

Maybe she was lonely.

Around the middle of November, at the height of the winter sales season, I went out for a meal with my boss.

Sales at San Dominico were below year-earlier levels, and the main reason was clear: I, the top salesman, was in a slump.

As the alcohol started to kick in, the boss began to regale me with war stories of the time when he had been a salesman. On the face of it, he was explaining to me forcefully that I would be unable to cross over, but now was not the time to be telling me anything like that. After all, this was the kind of business where people would steal the eyes from a live horse, and we had all heard, in endless repetition, all the legends of those who had trod these paths before us.

The boss was prefacing just about everything he said with phrases like "I'm not telling you to take it to that level..." and "It's not completely the same but..." But that was just every-day stuff for me. The truth was, the reason my sales had fallen off was exactly that: I had stopped taking it to that level.

For all I knew, the boss understood the whole picture, and what he was really saying was that I *should* be taking it to that level.

And the more he drank, the stupider the boss's lecture got.

That night, the boss was really drunk. I drove him in his Porsche toward his place in Setagaya. But on the way there, he said he wanted to spend the night at his girlfriend's.

He was half asleep in the passenger seat, and I had trouble understanding his mumbled directions, but finally we arrived at the woman's place in Hatsudai. The boss was none too steady on his feet as I dragged him up the stairs, and all I could think was, if the person who would put up with this drunk was the so-called designer, as was rumored at the office, how embarrassing this was going to be for all of us.

As we walked, I remember having this conversation:

"Boss, do you believe women are witches?"

"Huh…what do you mean, witches? If there was such a thing, I mean, how many times do you think I would have been killed already? I have no idea. What the hell are you talking about, anyway? Why'd you bring that up all of a sudden, out of nowhere? You're getting kind of creepy."

"Not at all. Just from listening to you, I can tell you've had all kinds of trouble in your life."

"And you think that might have something to do with witches? Well, I suppose it could. I mean, we earn our living from women, right? So if at least some of them don't hate us, we're not really doing our jobs."

The boss sat down in front of the apartment door. There was nothing else to do but ring the bell, and the door opened violently.

And there stood a worn-out, middle-aged woman who didn't look like the boss's type at all. At the other end of the paper-strewn hallway, a baby was crying.

The woman shrieked a piercing shriek, and all of a sudden started punching the boss in the head.

"What the— You hardly ever come around, and whenever you do you're always like this. I'm so sorry, are you from his company?"

I said yes, but after that I had no voice. As he was being dragged away by the collar, the boss pressed a ten thousand-yen note in my hand.

"Don't tell anyone," he said to me. "This place might just be part of the curse. Take my car. Don't hit anything."

The baby's cries were still ringing in my ears.

I would probably never get a second chance to drive the boss's Porsche to my heart's content. I drove around the night city with no particular destination in mind.

I could not figure out the boss's personal life. At the company there was this self-styled "designer" who was absolutely worthless. Once some secret rendezvous of his with some celebrity had been picked up by the weekly magazines. Then he had his house in Setagaya and this condo in Hatsudai where he sometimes went when he was drunk. No matter what kind of a lucky bastard of the industry he might be, it had been only five years since he had struck out on his own and started the company, and this was more than just an idle flirtation.

"This place might just be part of the curse," he had said. His face seemed contorted with fear. If this was what could happen if a neglected woman's resentment builds up, that she puts a spell on a man and twists his life inside out, that was even scarier than the vengeful ghosts of dead people.

On the windshield, I could see the reflections of the faces of scorned women.

And before I knew it, without knowing just how I had driven there, I found myself on that cobblestone slope scattered with ginkgo leaves.

I think it was the middle of the night. And right there in the middle of that carpet of yellow leaves, cyclamens were blooming like a row of red lanterns.

I stopped the car in the middle of the hill. Parked in front of the store was a van with a white logo on an indigo ground. It was a Boulogne vehicle. The store's sign was turned off, but there was a crack of light at the base of the shutter.

I was at my wit's end and freezing in the car. I was trying not to think, and I was chain-smoking. I sat there like that for a long time.

Kotani came out, his jacket draped over his shoulders. Then, following him, Shizuka Tachibana walked out in a beam of light. It was the first time I ever saw her with her hair down. She was wearing a cowl-neck sweater and corduroy trousers. I found myself unbelievably jealous of her outfit.

Through the car window the couple kissed goodbye.

The taillights disappeared over the top of the hill. Shizuka Tachibana lingered in front of the store. The sight of her back hurt me more than the kissing scene.

Moving the car ahead slowly, I pulled up beside her.

Outside the tinted window, I saw her blanch for a second. Or more precisely, her face took on the same white color as the car body.

I rolled down the window, and she breathed a sigh of relief.

"Nice car. Yours?"

"No, it's my boss's."

She got closer to the guardrail and inspected the car closely.

"Were you watching?"

She leaned over close to the window, smiling flirtatiously. Everything about her seemed different, her appearance, her behavior, and I had a terrible sense of betrayal. From her loose hair, I could smell Kotani's cologne.

"I wouldn't trust him too much if I were you. Has he asked you to write any IOUs lately? That could get you into trouble."

Shizuka Tachibana looked up at the sky for a while, as if she were counting the falling leaves.

"He told me the same thing about you, that I shouldn't trust you. He said you aren't a very good person. Is that so?"

Just like an older woman, Shizuka Tachibana looked straight at me and broke into a smile.

It could be that, seeing me in different circumstances, Kotani had been afraid, and that had influenced his opening moves. That said, that was the only time I ever criticized the way another man conducted his business, either before or since. And even then, I might not have said anything at all if I hadn't witnessed that distasteful scene.

A wintry wind came blowing down from the top of the hill.

"Don't you want to get in the car? You'll catch cold."

I didn't want to go into the shop, which I knew still smelled of Kotani. Shizuka Tachibana came around the front of the car, plowing through the fallen leaves, and got in the passenger side. As I put the car in gear, though, she laid her hand gently on mine, on the shift lever.

"Let's talk here," she said. "I don't like this car very much."

Turning off the noisy engine, I explained to her, as truthfully as I could, just what Kotani was trying to do to her. The entire time, the two of us stared up at the yellow slope, where it seemed that at any moment the title "FIN," like at the end of a French movie, would come rising up. It was a beautiful, if meaningless, image.

She seemed not in the least surprised. While there was no reason she shouldn't be surprised, she just wasn't the sort of woman who let all her emotions show on her face. She just sat there staring at the meaningless landscape that spread out in front of the windshield. She crossed and re-crossed her corduroy-clad legs and toyed with the collar of her cowl-neck sweater.

"What will you do now?"

"Nothing in particular," she muttered. And then she said something completely unexpected. "You know, something just like this happened to me once before. The house I got from my ex-husband was taken from me. I never was very smart, and I guess I just never learn. I don't know any other way to make a living though."

"Aren't you afraid?"

"I have nothing else left to lose."

"Things could still get worse."

"I don't care. Even if I think about it there's nothing I can do."

She leaned the seat back and looked away from me.

"You don't seem to be a bad sort."

"There are other places where I'm doing the same things. The same things Kotani is doing to you."

"And why did you never do those things to me?"

I wonder myself, I thought.

"Because I'm older than you?"

"No, that's not it. It's because you're pretty."

This whole time, her hand remained on top of mine. It was pleasantly cool to the touch.

Then I thought of something terrible. I thought...this person might be dead already. Kyara might be a ghost store, I thought.

I knew of a few boutiques that had been eaten alive by the manufacturers, and the owner had literally wrung her own neck.

But then, still gripping my hand, she said something even more dreadful.

"A woman's wrath can be a terrible thing. My ex-husband did not die an easy death."

I relaxed my fingers, and Shizuka Tachibana stroked the back of my hand as if to comfort me in my fright.

"You are all right. I want to thank you for looking out for me."

She sat upright and got out of the car. She passed over the guardrail as lightly as a falling leaf, and then tapped on the car window as if she had just remembered something.

Her hair, blown by the wind, brushed my eyes.

"I would like you to come back and retrieve your clothes before too long. And...say hi to your boss for me."

She was smiling like one of the mannequins in the show window.

I drove off as if making an escape. I looked in the rearview mirror, but she was nowhere to be seen. In the middle of the slope, among the fallen ginkgo leaves, were the red flowers, like the embers of a dying fire.

I do not believe there is such a thing as witches. Most men in this world are too cowardly to think about things like that. There was just one time, however, when I did believe in witches.

Kotani died on Christmas night.

He was on a rush delivery, and en route to Yokohama his car skidded off the side of the road and crashed. The car went up in flames, so fierce the entire load of party dresses and even the license plate were unrecognizable. The accident was so bad all three lanes of the Keihin Expressway were closed for the entire night.

According to credible rumors, only the aluminum Boulogne tags were left unburnt, and that was how they identified the body. But I didn't know anyone who actually saw this, and as stories go it seemed beyond likely.

The next night, the accident was the only thing everyone was talking about in the Nishi-Azabu bar. The unfunny joke somebody told was that he wanted his company to switch to silvery aluminum tags too.

Not a soul said anything about Kotani's underhanded business practices. Everyone was dead tired from the year-end sales season. But everyone knew that his accident had been more than a mere coincidence.

The economy was booming again, and every day it seemed another new clothing manufacturer was making its debut or some new boutique was opening. And then the same number of manufacturers would fail, and the boutiques would close their shutters for good.

The death of a salesman was commemorated for that one night, and then forgotten. The very next day, the indigo blue Boulogne vans were once again running all over Tokyo as if nothing had happened.

It was not long before I too had forgotten all about Kotani.

All of that happened a long time ago. I no longer remember where or how I spent New Year's that year. The first day I went back to work, unencumbered by a necktie, the boss yelled at me. Everyone had a good laugh at the self-styled designer, who was wearing a fancy kimono that did not suit her in the least.

The inspection room in the basement was chock-full of the first shipments of early spring items, and it was busy as a field full of flowers. We were all checking items against our shipping invoices and packing our cars full of pastel-colored suits. The manager was standing in front of a mountain of cardboard boxes filled with New Year's towels and yelling, "You all get it? You're not going out there just to give away towels and come back empty-handed! Get to work!"

The curtain was rising on the season that had no end. The freshly waxed light blue vans were all packed so full of product they looked like they might sink. One after the other, they headed up the ramp.

It was a cold day, rain mixed with sleet. I was stuck in a traffic jam on Aoyama-dori, wondering whether I should stop at Kyara. I had long since gotten all of our clothes out of there, and Kyara didn't owe us any money. The decision whether to pay a New Year's call was up to my personal feelings alone.

I went straight there. I had no intention of striking up any business. I just wanted to see Shizuka Tachibana again. At the foot of the winter-bleak hill, I fought with myself. It was as if no store of that description had ever been there. Perhaps it had all been a bad dream.

I climbed the cobblestone hill in first gear.

A silver gray van was parked there with its tailgate wide open. It was stuffed full of suits covered in plastic. There was the young salesman from Palm Tree, fashionably dressed. When he noticed me, he shrank back and bowed his head.

Shizuka Tachibana came out of the store, holding up a

red umbrella. I drove slowly right past the store, without even rolling down the window.

I wondered what would become of Kyara. Not that it was any of my business.

Shizuka Tachibana was wearing her usual silk satin dress with the large pleat, and her jet-black hair was tied up in an elegant chignon. I don't know what salesman had helped her pick out that dress, but on her it looked too good to be true. Without necklace and earrings, even better.

From under her red umbrella she watched me pass by. With that brief recognition, I passed Kyara and kept going.

I had a whole list of stores where I had to drop off clothes.

At the top of the hill, I braked for a minute and looked in the rearview mirror. The back of the car was filled with pastel-colored suits.

I think the dots of red I could see in the wet, foggy side mirror were cyclamen. Or maybe it was her umbrella as she still stood looking after me.

And that was the last I ever heard of Kyara.

The Festival
of Lanterns

Chieko had no home to go back to.

In more unfortunate times perhaps it was common, but these days it seemed to be an unusual situation, and she never spoke of it. She was also well aware of her own self-image as a modest and quiet person.

When she thought of the particulars, nothing about it seemed strange.

Her parents split up when she was still too young to understand much of what was going on. While they were fussing about custody rights, Chieko lived with her paternal grandparents. Before the agreement could be worked out, her parents each remarried, and they both seemed to be so content with their new partners they were happy to abandon their parental rights. As far as the law was concerned, her grandparents were now her parents.

This caused no real problems in terms of everyday life, and she was not unhappy. Her grandparents were still young, and they were respectable in the grand old Tokyo tradition. They looked so young no stranger would have any reason to doubt they were her actual parents.

Chieko knew nothing of her mother's whereabouts. While it is unlikely her grandparents were totally in the dark, they probably didn't tell Chieko simply because they had completely cut their ties to her mother.

Her father she saw once, at her grandmother's funeral. He had a nice-looking wife and two children with him, but he quarreled with her grandfather at the wake, and the next day at the funeral procession he was nowhere to be seen.

At that time her father had said to her, as no more than a social courtesy, "Look how big you've grown," or something like that, and in return she had given him a civil smile. Given the weight of the blank space of over ten years that had passed, it was all perfectly understandable: her father's clumsy greeting, her grandfather's unsmiling attitude, her father's obviously reluctant wife and children.

Chieko's grandmother died when she was in high school, and her grandfather died when she was in her third year of college.

When her grandfather died, the landlord of their old wooden house and the people in the neighborhood took care of the funeral. As the only relative, all she had to do was sit right next to the coffin.

It was a simple affair, but she found out later there were reasons behind all the care people put into it.

It was a miracle that the traditional *nagaya* wooden house had survived amid the urban valleys of office buildings in East Kanda, and now the landlord wanted to tear it down. It was just the time when land prices were skyrocketing, and the landlord had told all the tenants his terms for getting them out, which they were more than willing to do. But Chieko's grandfather had been the oldest tenant, and he had never consented. Of course, with land prices in this desirable, central part of Tokyo now in the tens of millions of yen per *tsubo*, it was only natural that the young landlord couple would be getting people together and making plans, doing everything they could to get their way.

On the way home from the crematorium, the other tenants all disappeared, whether by prior arrangement or not, and Chieko was treated to a meal in a French restaurant for the very first time in her life, just the three of them: the young landlord and his wife, and her.

When dessert was served, the landlord spread out the floor plan of a condominium building on the table. He spoke in his sweetest, nicest voice, like an old friend, but his message was blunt. Chieko could either accept a studio apartment on the seventh floor of the new building or a one million-yen payment to go away.

And of course the rent on the new apartment would be ten times as much as the rooms in the old wooden building. He said Chieko wouldn't have to pay a deposit or key money, but the rent alone was enough to convince her she should take her one million yen and find some other place to live.

Chieko was pretty sure the terms being offered to her were a different story from what the other tenants were getting. She knew she was being taken advantage of, but she had no idea how to fight back.

That was how Chieko lost her home.

The air conditioning in the *shinkansen* was too cold, and the cigarette smoke her husband was exhaling was hitting her right in the face. It seemed to Chieko that he was smoking more, but she wasn't brave enough to ask him not to. And of course it was all a matter of stress.

Around the time Mt. Fuji disappeared from view, she broke her silence. "When we get there, are you going to talk to your father and your brother about it?"

"Nah," he said, without lifting his face from his magazine.

"Listen to me. After the memorial service is over, and I don't care if they call it a 'family conference' or whatever, this whole discussion is going to be a real problem."

"They aren't going to do anything like that."

Chieko's husband stubbed out his cigarette and hurriedly lit another. She wondered how this small-minded man had ever become a surgeon. She had to admit his hands were very dexterous though.

"Your mother and father know, don't they?"

"My brother doesn't know."

"How could that be? I mean, they're living under the same roof!"

She knew better than to provoke her husband. They would never get back to a tranquil life at this point, but attacking his faults was not wise, as it merely caused him to get his back up.

But the fix they were in now was the direct result of being afraid and saying nothing when it had been important to say something.

"I'm sure your father is going to say something to me."

"Maybe. I'm sure he won't say anything bad."

"Of course not. I haven't done anything wrong."

His eyes, reading the magazine, were blank. He removed his glasses, looked up at the soft lighting of the first-class car, and puffed out smoke like a sigh.

"You should have brought that Ono woman instead of me. I bet that would have made everybody happy."

"Her due date is very soon. She couldn't have made the trip."

She bit down on her back tooth in a combination of anger and shame.

"Oh, so you did mean to bring her."

"Oops…No, that's not what I meant to say. You always twist things."

"I am not twisting things. Next year at this time, it'll be that Ono woman and her baby you'll be taking home with you."

He stole a glance at Chieko's profile. In the year since she had found out, it was an expedient measure that had become a habit. He was like a child caught in a lie and trying to cover it up.

"What will you do?"

"What should I do?"

Kaori Ono. Her husband's "woman." Chieko could barely bring herself to think of the name. She had been a nurse in the hospital where her husband worked, but by now of course she had quit.

Chieko knew Miss Ono's face only from a photograph. She was young, but not at all pretty. There was not that much difference in their ages, and Chieko was not ready to give up. Her husband was weak, and he had been snared by a slut. That was what Chieko had thought for a long time now, and though he said they had split up, that did not appear to be the case. Soon there would be a child, and it was clear where the responsibility lay.

("Mrs. Aoki. My name is Kaori Ono. I'm sure you've heard my name by now. I am pregnant with the doctor's baby, and I'm going to have it.")

Replaying that telephone conversation in her mind, Chieko had to close her eyes to stand the pain. Ever since, she had not been able to forget that cursed voice even for an instant. She had not had any other contact with Kaori Ono, neither before nor since. Chieko did not know anything about what sort of woman she was. And because she knew so little, her imagination was filling in the blanks.

"Chieko, this is the first O-bon since my grandfather died and the first time you've been to one of these at my family's, isn't it?" her husband said, trying to change the subject. "I should say this now, but the first O-bon in my family is as big a deal as the funeral. Just so you know."

"So you're saying people won't have the time to be trading gossip?"

"That's right. The monk comes, and everyone chants the sutras, and everybody from the whole town comes bearing gifts. You'll be surprised, you'll see."

"Nothing would surprise me anymore."

Her husband was doing his best to keep the conversation going his way.

"My grandfather really liked you. You remember when we got married? He even tried to follow you when you went to change your clothes, saying 'Wow, a college-educated bride sure is something different.' Afterward, that's all he could talk about, and my brother's wife got her knickers all in a twist about it."

If her husband's grandfather were still alive, what would he make of the situation they found themselves in now? For the last few years of his life he had been unable to get out of bed, so he probably hadn't heard anything about it.

Chieko didn't really know if she had been any particular favorite of his, but he had been kind to her even though she had no relatives of her own. The fact that her marriage had gone bad probably also had something to do with the fact that he was such an important man. He was from a wealthy farming family with a history of public service in the region, and he had been a six-term member of the city council.

At their wedding, he acted as a member of her family and sat with her young women friends on the bride's side.

"What's this? Here I am with enough gravitas for ten people," he had said, laughing. It was he who accepted the flowers customarily given to the bride's parents. Chieko's only merit was that she had graduated from the pharmacology department of a national university, but her groom's grandfather had made sure that everybody knew about it.

"Come to think of it, you were raised by your grandfather, weren't you," her husband said, smiling and coughing smoke, trying to keep the conversation on track. Chieko looked away, evading his glance, and turned her attention to the passing landscape, burning in the summer sun.

As if you knew anything about my grandfather, she thought to herself.

Her husband had warned her not to be surprised at the grand scale of the first O-bon ceremonies that were customary in his hometown, which went well beyond what was done in Tokyo.

Her husband's family home was in the middle of an expansive tea field, without even a stand of trees to break the wind. It was a vast piece of land that seemed to go on and on without end.

There was a fence around the house itself, and all along the fence were wreaths of flowers, just as there had been at the funeral. Chieko could hardly believe her eyes. So this was how they marked a first O-bon here in the countryside.

The county road was one long line of parked cars. The yard and the gate area were filled with people. She could hardly tell the difference from the funeral six months before.

As they got out of the taxi, a family in funeral dress emerged from a station wagon parked in front of the gate.

"My older sister's family from Nagoya. We should say hello," her husband whispered in her ear as he wiped the sweat from his brow.

"Your sister from Nagoya?"

"Yes, my older brother's wife."

"Oh? Your sister-in-law brought her whole family?"

As a daughter-in-law herself, her position in the family was the same as her sister-in-law's. Chieko was a bit bewildered, and her husband said to her, meanly, "You don't have any family to bring, even if I had asked you to."

"I've never seen anything like this in Tokyo. Even if it is the first O-bon since your grandfather died, I just can't believe your sister-in-law brought her whole family."

Her husband looked doubtfully at Chieko. "You shouldn't say things like that, even by mistake. What does it matter what people do in Tokyo? You are an Aoki now. You should apologize."

Amid the tumult of the household, Chieko suddenly lost

her nerve. How should she apologize? *I'm so sorry, I have no relatives of my own...* Would she have to run around saying things like that to all the assembled members of her husband's extended family?

"In Tokyo, the seventh-day observance is usually done at the same time as the funeral itself. The forty-nine-day memorial is usually just for close relatives. And the first O-bon is just family."

They stood at the gate, and Chieko's husband grabbed her hand, more roughly than necessary.

"Stop saying things like that. Who cares what people in Tokyo do? You are a daughter of this household. Besides, when we got married, everybody learned everything there is to know about you."

The front garden was filled with floral wreaths, all the way to the open back garden. The wood-and-paper sliding doors had been removed from the big room that faced the garden, and deep in the room, where the sunlight didn't reach, was the same Buddhist altar that had been there for the funeral. It was a magnificent altar, with gaudy gold and silver drapery and urns of flowers, but no casket. The altar was covered with the same kinds of decorations that were there for the funeral: Chieko's husband's grandfather's photograph, condolence cards, medals and trophies.

The people who had entered the house, in their funeral clothes, were exchanging showy greetings.

"Brother, we are here. Sorry to be late," Chieko's husband, suddenly lapsing into broad dialect, called to his older brother. His brother was preoccupied with other guests farther into the room, but his wife came out to the edge of the garden to greet them.

"Ah, Kuni. And Chieko. How good you could come. We were just wondering when you would get here. The priest will arrive soon. Honey! Kunio is here. They're here!"

Kunio's brother waved his hand from the back of the

room. "Hey, glad you could make it. You were late, so we started to get worried about the time. We're going to start at four, so hurry up and change."

"It's been a while," Chieko said, but so quietly it was impossible to know whether her husband's brother heard her or not. And then he was enclosed again within the circle of guests. Chieko felt everyone was looking at her out of the corner of their eye.

But she also felt that her brother-in-law was avoiding her gaze altogether.

"Use the second floor of the storehouse. You'll be able to spend the night?"

"We plan to, but is it okay? I mean, we could stay in a hotel in Hamamatsu."

"No, don't worry about that. You live the farthest away of anybody. For almost everybody else it's a day trip. They'll all be back for the bonfire on the final day."

"Yeah, we'll have to miss that. I hope you don't mind. I'm needed at the hospital."

"Yeah, sure. Maybe just Chieko could come down," her sister-in-law said, as if it was obvious that was what she should do.

Bonfires were lit on the first night of O-bon to welcome the spirits of the dead and again on the last night to send them back where they belonged. This was a custom that was not unknown in Tokyo, but it was no longer practiced.

"What's going on?" Chieko asked, looking up at her husband. This reveling would likely go on for the full length of the O-bon festival. It seems the whole clan was expected to be here for everything, from the first bonfire to the last.

Her husband saw the distressed look on her face and realized he had to talk his way out of this.

"Sorry, I didn't think about that. We weren't thinking we would stay that long. Don't you have to go back to work yourself?"

He winked one eye so that his sister-in-law wouldn't see.

"It's not that we wouldn't be able to do it somehow. The trip can be done in a day on the *shinkansen*," Chieko chimed in, thwarting her husband's attempt to sidestep.

"Chieko, maybe you could make the trip back down by yourself. Our grandfather always really liked you. I know you're busy though."

"I'll do my best to be here."

"Well, I hope that means you'll be here if you can. All the other relatives will be here, with their children."

Her sister-in-law's words had barbs of their own.

The room on the second floor of the storehouse had been remodeled for overnight guests. There was nothing they could do about the smell of mold, but at least the air conditioner worked well. As they changed into their funeral clothes, Chieko's husband expressed his annoyance.

"Why couldn't you just have said you have to work and left it at that? It's not exactly easy to find a substitute pharmacist. Didn't you say you had to go to a lot of trouble to arrange the rotation so you could make the trip here today? You think you'll be able to come back again?"

"I'll see what I can do. Your grandfather always liked me, and I don't have any children."

He was tying his necktie in the mirror, but his hands came to an abrupt halt. She hadn't meant anything particularly negative by that remark, but it was a time when they were each seeing demons in the other's words.

"I'll go on ahead. Will you be able to finish dressing on your own?"

"I can take care of it myself," she said bluntly, holding the rope of her *obi* in her teeth. Her husband was already descending the steep, squeaky ladder staircase.

The storehouse had no glass windows. With the bare light bulb glowing in the mirror, she couldn't see well enough to pencil her eyebrows. There was a small window in the stairwell, but it was plastered up and looked like it hadn't been opened in a hundred years.

But when she stood at the top landing and reached up to open the latch, she found it opened surprisingly easily. The sunlight came into the room.

Shading her eyes with her sleeve, she could see across a broad landscape of tea bushes in neatly groomed rows. What a vast, fertile plantation, she thought to herself.

She recalled the time, six years before, when she had first accompanied Kunio, as his girlfriend, on a visit to this place. It seemed strange to her at the time, but now she could see how this plot of earth had nurtured Kunio, who was otherwise so unworldly. Not a speck of gloom, just a big, boundless, well-ordered tea plantation. It was a landscape like a painted picture, fertile, but at the same time somehow meaningless.

From beneath the persimmon tree below the window, Chieko could hear low voices. She could see the heads of her husband and her father-in-law through the gaps in the leaves.

"Well, Kunio, what are you going to do? You may be too old for a parent to butt in, but your child is about to be born, and I don't see as I have any other choice. I feel bad for Chieko, marrying into the family and never having a child, but the family can't survive that way. I don't see what's so difficult about it. If it's just a matter of money we can do something about that. She'll understand."

"Dad, that might make sense here, but in Tokyo there are couples who deliberately never have children."

"How can that be? I mean think about your own situation. You'll open your own practice someday. What will you do if you have no one to succeed you?"

"Be that as it may, it's not something I will ever say. 'You won't have a baby, so I'm going to divorce you.' In Tokyo that logic would not be convincing to anyone."

"That's why I told you time and again not to settle down

with a Tokyo girl. What I want to know is, how come somebody you love and have been with for six years hasn't had a
baby by now?"

"It's not that she can't, she just hasn't. She says she won't
have a baby because she has to work until she pays off her
student loans."

"What is that supposed to mean? These Tokyo college girls, they're so shameless, they get so they can't have
babies."

"That's ridiculous. Besides, she never knew another man
before me. I'm sure of it."

"Just don't go to court or anything like that. Talk to her
and make some kind of agreement. If it's money, we'll come
up with something."

"Dad, I'm telling you I still have a problem with this.
Chieko and I, we've always had trouble seeing eye to eye."

The voices faded as her husband and father-in-law walked
away toward the main house.

Chieko quietly closed the window and descended from
the landing. She wondered when her husband would choose
to broach the subject of divorce with her. If she didn't bring
it up, she doubted he would be able to either.

She shifted the position of the mirror and tentatively tried
once more to pencil her eyebrows. She wondered about lipstick and decided her face without a touch of red was simply
too forlorn.

Looking at herself in the mirror, she muttered to herself
without thinking the same phrase she had always used, since
she was a child, at times like this: "Pull yourself together."

This had always worked for her, and it made her feel
confident that nothing bad would happen this time either. A
man who had hardly been able to bring himself to propose to
her was likely to have just as much trouble saying he wanted
a divorce.

The monk arrived in grandiose finery.

Over a brown silk gauze robe he wore an elaborate golden cope and a large golden hat. Five or six young monks accompanied him, carrying bells and gongs and other religious paraphernalia.

The wood-and-paper dividers had been removed from the four quarters of the big room, which was now packed with people in funeral dress. It had been frightfully hot during the day, but now that the sun was down a cool breeze blew, and it had become a comfortable summer evening.

Once the long sutra chanting and the bell ringing performance were over, little printed books of sutras were handed out to the assembly, who were all to recite the sutras together. This too was a custom that would have been unthinkable in Tokyo.

The monk went to another room, and Chieko's father-in-law stood before the altar.

"I want to thank you all for coming. The time has come for us to light the fires that greet the spirits. While we do that, a meal will be set out here, so we hope you can all stay for a while before you have to go."

People were joking with one another about their feet falling asleep, and everybody was making their way into the evening garden. No one was giving directions, but people somehow formed a long line from the gate to the front door of the main building of the house for the greeting fires.

At the gate facing the county road, a torch would be lit, and from there the flame would pass to small bundles of pine branches that lined the path every two or three steps. Forming a broad arc across the spacious yard, it created a path for the spirits to tread.

Chieko watched the others to see how it was done, and built her own little pile of wood, like building blocks.

"Ready? I'm going to light it!" her father-in-law yelled from the gate, and then the flame began to be passed from the gate onward. The piles that had sapwood flared up in an amusing dance. One at a time, the small flames flickered up against the evening darkness.

"So, Grandpa's spirit is going to see this, and it'll show him where to come, from wherever he is, right?" her husband said as he crouched on the ground blowing on his little flame.

"I wonder where they do come from?"

"I wonder too."

Chieko took a spark from the fire her husband was holding out to her and lit her own at her feet. She had to blow only once and the flame sprang up.

In the kitchen, women in their formal funeral dress were working hard.

"I have to go help."

"It's all right," her husband said, standing up and tugging at Chieko's sleeve. "There are a lot of people coming, but it's not as busy as the funeral was. Everybody has to stop at many homes for O-bon, so most will just have a ritual drink and move on."

Chieko saw it was so. The people who had attended the greeting fire went to the big room, had one small glass of sake, and left. Then new guests came, walking along the path marked by the greeting fire.

Most of the people who came to read the sutras and light the greeting fire with the family were near neighbors and close friends. Another wave of O-bon guests would come later in the evening for the bonfire.

They too would step up into the big room from the edge of the garden, offer up a stick of incense, have a ritual drink of sake, and leave.

"This year there's five households celebrating first O-bon right here in this area. Just to visit those five would take all night," her sister-in-law said, adding more fuel to one of the fires.

"I should go in and help, shouldn't I?" Chieko asked.

"No, you don't have to. There's already a bunch of women in the kitchen gossiping up a storm. You'd just get your feelings hurt. What's a person to do? About Kunio, I mean."

So saying, her sister-in-law looked daggers at Chieko's husband, who was sitting on the ground hugging his knees like a child, staring at the fire, and she went back into the kitchen.

"She sure was nasty."

"Seems it's not a secret anymore."

Chieko's husband did not respond.

For all that there seemed to be hardly any houses in this village, such a never-ending line of people came to visit for O-bon that one had to wonder where they all lived.

The county road was a ceaseless stream of cars. Along the ridges in the tea fields that went on and on behind the house, the light of flashlights moved around like fireflies.

Chieko's husband stepped up into the main room and got lost in the crowd. At a loss for where to go, Chieko sat quietly by herself and kept feeding twigs to the fire.

Staring at the flame, Chieko wondered why she was doing this. She had always been able to manage for herself, and she enjoyed the freedom of living alone. She was not as unhappy as people might imagine. So why was she suffering every day, feeling trapped in a living hell, struggling like a bug caught in a spider's web? Did she have to be here, enduring the stares and whispers of all these people around her, taking part in these unfamiliar customs?

A human silhouette loomed above the flame she was tending, and she looked up. There stood her father-in-law and her brother-in-law, short and stout, like two melons in a patch. Each stood there looking down at Chieko, waiting for the other to speak first.

These two men were both quite different from her husband, who was tall and slender, but all three of them had the same indecisiveness.

After a moment's hesitation, her father-in-law suddenly said something horrible.

"How come none of your relatives are here, Chieko?" He had a carefully arranged little smile that was similar to her husband's. He wasn't being disagreeable, he was just taking a very circuitous route to telling Chieko she wasn't really the right person to be part of the family. That she never had been.

Smiling the same smile, her brother-in-law said, "You know, Chieko, since you went to college, maybe you're not happy being just a housewife. Job or family? Lots of people have to make that choice. If you're both working, you'll never be able to make a baby. You can't just blame Kunio for that."

Her father-in-law was doing his best with a bad hand, but her brother-in-law was being a coward, she thought to herself. It was this same brother-in-law who had been the first to stick up for her, because wouldn't it be great when Kunio opens his own practice if his wife was a pharmacist?

In a gruff manner unsuited to the time and place, Chieko stood up without thinking and raised her voice, saying, "What you mean to say is you'd prefer a nurse to a pharmacist?"

The two men looked at each other and exchanged a surprised glance. Like her husband, they were completely unaccustomed to arguing. But from the way they feigned surprise, she could tell they both knew all the details.

"It was always my plan to be just a housewife once I finish paying off my student loans. I didn't want to burden Kunio with my debts."

"I understand that, but do you see how that might be awkward for Kunio?" her brother-in-law asked, still smiling.

"Well, I certainly never meant to make Kunio feel awkward. Why don't you ask him what exactly has been so awkward?"

"He never has been able to express himself very well. That's why his family members are so worried about him. As a scholar yourself, surely you understand that."

"This is our problem to deal with as a couple. We've been talking about it."

As if her words had somehow touched a nerve, the smile disappeared from her father-in-law's face and was replaced by a serious, even threatening look.

"Kunio's been living on pins and needles every day. You think we can just ignore that? If you have a problem with family members getting involved, why don't you just bring your family around and we'll talk about it? The two of you will never be able to work through this on your own," her father-in-law said scornfully.

"Dad, you can't go saying things like that. You know that even if she wanted to, she has no family members to bring," her brother-in-law said, in an effort to calm his father. For a moment, Chieko thought the two of them had carefully worked out this whole conversation in advance, like a skit.

Her brother-in-law placed his hand on his father's sleeve and said, feigning sympathy, "Parental concern, don't worry about that. How could anyone expect you to understand? What I mean is, our two families can't get together and discuss this on equal footing, so it ends up kind of a one-way thing, which is too bad. We want to do what we can to help you get past this. Chieko, don't think badly of us. Hear what we have to say."

So that's how it was.

Chieko's whole body shook with an anger she had no place to put.

"I see," was all she said. What she meant was that she would go along with the conversation. The two men exhaled simultaneously in relief, as if she had already agreed to a divorce.

Chieko imagined a conversation in which she was

surrounded by the whole clan. She was all alone, unable even to speak up for justice. She had not done a single thing wrong. This was all completely irrational. If only she had even one real relative, no matter how distant. If only there were someone who would speak up for her case, imagine how much braver that would make her, even if the result were the same.

The wind died down, and the smoke from the greeting fires coiled at the edge of the garden. Chieko dabbed her eyes with her handkerchief, as if she had gotten smoke in them. *If you let them see you cry you're a loser*, she thought to herself. She felt a moan in her throat, but she bit it back. Her body felt weak. She crouched beside the greeting fire.

She thought she heard someone call her name: "Chiiko." In the embers of the fire near the gate, she thought she could see a little silhouette.

"Chiiko."

"Yes," she responded, before she could even think.

"Chiiko."

It had been her childhood nickname.

The silhouette came through the gate as if emerging from a darkened picture frame and walked through the smoke that was lit faintly by the greeting fires.

"Chiiko."

This time Chieko did not answer but just looked all around her. There was no reason that anyone here would be calling her by that name.

"What's this? A relative of Chieko's?" her father-in-law asked, curiously. Her brother-in-law, trying to wave the smoke away, squinted at the silhouette.

Chieko started to say no, but her lips froze. "Grandpa…"

There was her grandfather. He wore a black suit like all the other O-bon well-wishers. Her grandfather had come.

"Grandfather? You mean, *your* grandfather?"

More than surprise, what she felt stuck in her throat was

simply joy. Wiping the tears from her face, she nodded again and again.

"Yes, it's my grandfather. My grandfather came, as a favor to me."

"Well, I must say…"

Her father-in-law and brother-in-law drew back as if to clear the way.

Her grandfather, who never was a big man, held his head high as he came walking from the gate down the path of fire. Even the way he walked, throwing his feet wide to each side, had not changed.

He came up to where Chieko's father-in-law and brother-in-law were standing and courteously bowed his pure white, close-cropped head. He bowed formally, from the waist, like a yakuza gangster. Once, Chieko had been very embarrassed when he bowed the same way to her elementary school teacher at a parents' meeting.

"I must apologize for my late arrival. I believe this is the first time we have met. I am Chieko's grandfather."

Chieko's father-in-law and brother-in-law mumbled in confusion some formal words of greeting.

"For various reasons, I am forced to live somewhat apart. My humble apologies for being out of touch."

Her father-in-law said, "Not at all. We are honored that you are here. Chieko neglected to mention that you would be coming. Chieko! You see! Your grandfather is here. If you had called from the train station, we would have sent someone to meet you."

"Not at all," her grandfather said, bending his small body and waving his knobby workman's hand. "I haven't been able to do much for my granddaughter, so there's no reason you should be sending someone to pick me up."

"You seem to have found the house just fine on your own."

"With all these fine and powerful greeting fires burning,

anybody would be able to find this place. I must say, this is a magnificent home you have here. I had heard some rumors to that effect. Chieko is very lucky."

Her grandfather still spoke in his old-fashioned Tokyo way, keeping his gaze fixed on the two men. It was as if he had heard of his granddaughter's unhappiness and come riding to her rescue.

Chieko too was staring intently at her grandfather, illuminated by the greeting fires.

Even if it's a dream it's okay. I'm sure it's a dream, she thought to herself.

"Grandpa."

Her grandfather turned to look at her, smiling. He was poor and he liked to drink, and he never learned to read and write to his own satisfaction, but he hated when things were out of whack. His smile was just the best.

"Stop crying. Your grandfather is here now. Everything is all right. You don't have to cry," her grandfather said loudly so everyone could hear.

Her father-in-law and brother-in-law had probably been hoping they could just take care of this matter before the night was through, but now they recoiled before a formidable opponent they had not foreseen. Still smiling, Chieko's grandfather returned his gaze to them.

"I hear you're all very fond of my granddaughter."

"Oh...grandfather. Please, first light a stick of incense."

"Of course. I have come a long way to be here at your first O-bon celebration. Let's save the more complicated discussion for later, shall we? A stick of incense, please."

Chieko's grandfather stepped over the greeting fires and walked to the veranda.

Chieko's father-in-law wiped the sweat from his brow. "Chieko," he said, "why didn't you tell us...?"

"Is something wrong? Just a few minutes ago you were saying I should have brought some relatives."

"No, it's just that I hadn't heard anything about your grandfather."

"So if my grandfather's here, does that make some sort of a difference?

"Not especially. That's not what I'm saying at all."

For a moment, the to-do in the big room was silent. Chieko's brother-in-law announced the arrival of her grandfather, and her husband bolted up from his seat at the party. He pushed past other people in the room to reach the edge of the garden, and even from a distance anyone could see he was as white as a sheet.

"Well hello there, Kunio," the grandfather said in a loud, grand voice, just as Kunio reached the narrow veranda.

"Ku...Kuni...?? Chieko! What's going on here?"

This was not good. Of all the people in the gathering, only Kunio would recognize her grandfather's face. On her desk at home she had a photograph of him wearing a *happi* coat.

Chieko came up behind her grandfather. Her husband was clinging to a post, his narrow eyes grown wide. His knees were knocking.

"Grandfather has come. Won't you say hello?"

"He...hello. So glad you could come. You...what exactly is going on here? I don't understand."

"It is O-bon."

Chieko's husband sat down on the threshold. An uncomfortable silence spread through the room. Many of the people there were certainly thinking this was a proud relation come to press the attack against the husband for the wrong he had done in Tokyo. Those who secretly knew all the facts of the matter could do little to object. All they could do was hang their heads.

Opening his mouth as if he were about to sing some workman's chantey, her grandfather said in a resonant voice, "Listen here, everyone. I am very sorry to be disturbing your peaceful evening. Please don't mind me."

Everyone resumed drinking as if to avoid any further contact with Chieko's grandfather.

He removed his shoes and arranged them neatly on the ground before stepping up to the veranda. He spoke into the ear of Kunio, who still sat quaking and clinging to the post. "Say, Kunio."

"Ye...yes."

"Just what do you think you're doing, playing my grand-daughter for a fool."

"A fool? I don't know what you're talking about."

"You come along and think you can convince people black is white. Listen, I came a long way to be here. Speak up for yourself."

"About what, do you mean?"

"We'll have time to go over this in detail later, but depend-ing on what you say right now I might be taking you back with me. And everybody else in your family too."

"Wha...what? You must be joking."

"It would be no trouble at all. A car accident on the Tomei Expressway could be arranged. Or perhaps I shouldn't waste any time and just burn this house down right now."

All of a sudden, Chieko's husband fell to the ground in the garden and bowed so vehemently he hit his forehead hard on the ground.

"I'm sorry! I'm so sorry. Please forgive me!"

Everyone in the room remained silent. Chieko's grandfa-ther glanced back at the dumbfounded crowd and smiled an embarrassed smile.

"There, there now, Kunio. I don't care how many mis-takes you've made, a big man doesn't act like an idiot. And in front of the dead no less."

Grandfather is absolutely the best, Chieko thought.

Chieko never learned the details of that night's talk, which went on until the eastern sky turned pale white.

Her grandfather did not let her listen in because he said

the conversation could not progress in the presence of a crying woman. She spent the entire night sitting on a bench in the garden, playing with a puppy. Although the rain shutters were in place, from time to time she could hear the serious voices of the men.

When all the talking was done and her grandfather emerged through the front door, there was a bright white morning fog on the tea fields. Her grandfather was as tired as could be.

"Chiiko. I've talked this through for you. You don't have to say anything more."

It must have been quite a discussion. No one came out to see Chieko's grandfather off.

Unbuttoning the front of his jacket and loosening his necktie, he walked slowly along the path of the burned-out greeting fires.

"Your husband is not such a bad man. This whole business is regrettable, a simple matter of temptation. Speaking of which, do you still love him?"

Chieko stood up and thought for a minute. She could not lie to her grandfather. But before she could say out loud that she still loved her husband, her grandfather heaved a sigh.

"Is that so. I'm sorry. But listen here, Chiiko. The thing is, Kunio, the rat, has no feelings for you anymore...What was that name again?"

"Kaori Ono..."

"That's it. The young nurse. He's infatuated with her. These countryside millionaires. They don't always think through the consequences of their actions. You're better off making a clean break."

This conclusion took Chieko by surprise, and she lifted her head. Her grandfather's eyes were sad.

"That's an awful thing to say. Grandfather, what did you come here for? I haven't done anything wrong. And now you're saying I'm the one who should back down. I don't get it."

"Not back down. He's not good enough for you. I told him you didn't need a single cent of his money. I feel so much better already."

"Well, I don't. What have you done? This is terrible!"

Chieko was about to go back into the big room, but he grabbed her arms. His hands, touching her upper arms in their funeral kimono, were quite warm.

Her grandfather looked intently at her, and his big mouth trembled. Her grandfather was crying.

"What? Why are you crying?"

"Why are you saying things like that to me? You would say that to a spirit who came to visit you on O-bon?"

"Don't you see? I don't understand! You never told me anything that wasn't true, and you never lost to anyone. That's why I've always tried so hard."

"That's true. You have always tried so hard."

Every day since her grandfather died weighed on Chieko like demons on her back. For the very first time, Chieko could see how she had suffered.

"The truth is, I always wanted to be a doctor. I..."

Realizing she had fallen in love with her husband through a mistake that could not be reversed, she reached out and clung to her grandfather.

"I'm afraid I always liked to drink too much. I was never much use to you."

"Grandfather, tell me. Why must I split up with my husband?"

Her grandfather hesitated a moment before speaking. His thin voice rasped like a wintry wind in Chieko's ear.

"It would be wrong, pitiful even, to bring a child into the world without parents. This I know better than anyone."

Chieko, at a loss for a response, cried on her grandfather's chest.

"Chiiko, I hope you can understand. When I died, that was the only thing I could think about. Above all, I was worried about leaving you alone and unhappy in the world."

"But you did nothing wrong. It was my mother and father who were wrong."

Her grandfather lifted Chieko's shoulders and stroked her head with his big hands, the way he always had when he returned from work long ago. He looked over his shoulder at the ridges in the tea fields, now cloaked in deep fog.

"Uh-oh. I'm late getting back, and now he's here."

In the fields, they could see a human silhouette emerging from the fog.

"Who is that?"

"Your husband's grandfather. He's a peculiarly conscientious sort. I explained to him that I felt a responsibility toward you, so he let me take his place for a night. By rights, though, this was *his* first O-bon. I took advantage of him."

"Give him my best regards. He always liked me."

Her grandfather smiled and turned on his heel. As he passed through the gate, he looked up at the detailing and gave a snort of laughter.

"Shoddy work. The carpenters must have been country bumpkins."

Finally, her grandfather's form was swallowed up by the fog. Chieko waved her hand to the two balls of light that floated up above the tea fields.

That day, Chieko's husband went back to Tokyo without saying a word to her.

Perhaps he had no intention of returning to their apartment, where her grandfather's photo and memorial tablet were. No matter. The jealousy was erased from Chieko's heart as if it had never been there.

She spent the whole day lazily in the second-floor room of the storehouse.

She had a lot to think about. Without alimony, she had just enough of her own money to get by for a little while.

Perhaps she should just pack her bags and get out. Or maybe she should try to get the apartment at least.

Pharmacists were always in demand, and there would be no reason she would have to leave her long-term workplace even if she got divorced.

Yesterday's despair had given way to today's hope. She was still only thirty.

A few O-bon visitors were still arriving at the house, but not as many as yesterday. At noon, as if walking on eggshells, her sister-in-law brought lunch on a tray.

"Chieko, you know you don't have to stick around for the send-off fires. You have to work, don't you? You can go home. Father said so."

Her sister-in-law sat at the top of the steep staircase and set down the lunch and the tea service.

"Mind if I eat my lunch here too?"

"Not at all. I'm happy to eat with you."

Her sister-in-law nibbled at her food as if she had little appetite.

Her sister-in-law said quietly, "Chieko, I admire you."

"Really, why? I never had a baby, I never looked after my husband well enough. I'm not very good at my wifely duties."

Her sister-in-law set down her chopsticks and dabbed at her eyes with her handkerchief.

"The men of this family are all so stubborn. They have no humility, but really they all owe you an apology. I hope you can forgive them."

"It seems last night's discussion got quite heated. My grandfather can be quite stubborn himself."

"Stubborn? Your grandfather? I wonder."

Chieko's sister-in-law poured the tea, then listlessly turned her eyes, swollen from crying, toward the ceiling.

"Your grandfather is a good man. Looking at him I felt so sorry for him, so sorry."

"He must've seemed pretty threatening."

"Not really. But he really defended you whenever the conversation was moving in a direction that wasn't good for you. He would steer things away from divorce. He pleaded with Kunio to continue living with you. And he cried and cried…"

"My grandfather did?"

"Anybody can see the fault lies entirely with Kunio, so the family's side didn't have much to say. But that only makes them all the more stubborn, and they just clam up. I think it's inexcusable. Your grandfather kept it going all night long. At the very end he raised his voice, crying, and he said, 'Please, please, I won't ever be able to appear to you again.' He said it was the one wish of his life. Never before have I thought the men of this family to be so cold and heartless. I'm just about at the end of my rope with them."

Chieko closed her eyes hard and sipped her piping hot tea.

"Was my grandfather drinking sake?"

"No, he said he can't drink any alcohol. Is he ill? His face was kind of pale. Chieko, tell me the truth. Are you really okay with this? It seems so unfair to me."

"It's all right. I never minded living alone, and I've been able to spend six years with someone I love. I'm content with that."

Her sister-in-law sat and cried and said nothing for a while. Then she piped up, "Tonight, they'll be floating the little lantern boats on the beach. You should go see it. There'll be fireworks too."

"What are lantern boats?"

"The lantern boats for the dead to sail away. Don't you do that in Tokyo?"

Chieko thought she should see this before going back to Tokyo. Perhaps, just perhaps, she would be able to see her grandfather one more time.

The floating lantern boats of Sakihama were an ancient custom at O-bon. Her husband had described it to her once. Countless numbers of paper lanterns are released on the river in endless waves, heading for Potalaka, the sacred mountain of the Pure Land, out past the horizon of the sea. He said it was beautiful, like a dream.

Before leaving, Chieko was careful to say goodbye to every family member. The only one to look her straight in the eye was the photograph of Kunio's grandfather. As she looked at his cheeky smile—such a complete contrast to her own grandfather—Chieko covered her face with her hands and cried. Just as she was convincing herself this was the last time she would allow herself to feel miserable, she burst out in uncontrollable sobs, ignoring the stares of those around her.

Perhaps because someone had told her to, only her sister-in-law went with Chieko, carrying a paper lantern boat.

At a teahouse along the way, Chieko and her sister-in-law drank lukewarm beer. The fireworks were fired from a raft just offshore, painting the sky above the beach in an uninterrupted stream.

"I don't know if it's too late to be saying this. I don't want to hurt your feelings, Chieko, but I think things have turned out for the best. All the men in this family—my husband, his father, Kunio—they're all alike. I'm even a little jealous of you."

They made their way through the crowd at the mouth of the river to launch their paper lantern boat. Chieko slipped off her wedding ring and gently set it on board.

"We may never see each other again, but you're still young. You might still find the right person for you. Wouldn't that be nice, Chieko?"

Her sister-in-law's face was beautiful in the light of the paper lanterns.

The two of them walked along the beach, following the lantern boats as they floated out on the tide amid a million points of light reflected on the waves.

"It's really just a kind of littering. They collect all the boats again just a little ways offshore. It's really just a show for the kids."

Chieko didn't agree. In the stern of one of those boats, heading out to sea, sat her grandfather, snug in his *happi* coat.

Standing on tiptoes at the water's edge, Chieko cried "Grandfather!" The waves washed over her feet.

Just as he used to do in the crowds at Ryogoku's annual river-opening festival, her grandfather looked up at the fireworks blossoming in the night sky and clapped his hands at one particularly impressive blast.

"Grandpa! Look at me!"

Her grandfather showed no sign of noticing Chieko's shouting. He looked up at the sky where the fireworks were falling and glittering in a spectacular display and lifted up his fine, spirited, old-fashioned Tokyo voice.

At festivals and fireworks, he was enraptured, just like a child. Now as ever.

The soles of his *tabi* socks were always gleaming white.

At the public bath, he never hid his tattoos, even though they frightened some people. He did, however, always put a towel over the scar on his left shoulder from the wound he had suffered in the war. He would sit cross-legged on the tiles and wash Chieko behind the ears and between her toes, until it hurt.

No matter how drunk he was when he came home, he always woke up before Chieko and made her lunch. Chieko never tasted bread until after she graduated from high school.

She asked him not to wear his dirty traditional canvas shoes when he came to the school for parents' night, and even when he came to sports events he always wore a clean pair.

At her graduation ceremony he shouted, "Banzai!" for her at the school gate. When she was accepted at college, he wheeled around the whole neighborhood on a bicycle.

She still thought he was the best there could ever be.

"Grandpa! Grandpa! Over here!"

He did not look back. His boat, along with many other paper lantern boats surrounded by the reflected reds and blues of the fireworks on the sea, floated away.

Up to her ankles in the waves, Chieko suddenly felt she would like to have a baby.

Just as the kerchief wrapped around her grandfather's neck disappeared into the darkness, this was the thought that came rising up within her like a flame from deep inside her chest.

No-Good
Santa

It was Christmas Eve when Santa Kashiwagi's indictment was suspended and he was released from jail.

This was not just some pun on the prosecutor's part. With just a few business days left in the year, Santa was more of a chump than a criminal and a drain on the prison system's resources.

His mother came down to the jail to get him. Still in her office cleaning lady's uniform, she sat comfortably enough in the steel chair in the guardroom.

Even Santa felt a little pang in his chest. His mother was used to this by now, but seeing him again she made a show of lecturing him for the guards' sake.

Who did he think he was, thirty years old now already and a big man, still doing things that got him into trouble with the police? A year or two in the pen might do him some good, cool his head. He was too half-assed to even get sent to prison properly. More's the pity.

The truth was, his mother had only really bothered to lecture him when he was a teenager. Since he turned twenty, she was just going through the motions.

The detective on duty smiled a grim smile and said, "It's Christmas Eve, Santa. This is your busiest time of year. Isn't it, Mom?"

Santa's mother apparently didn't catch the hint of disgust

behind the little jest. She could think of three times this year alone she had had to come down to this very place and bow her head obsequiously to this same vice detective.

"No, I'm going to make him go right home and say his prayers right through 'til morning. I don't care if it is Christmas. After getting let off like this, if he thinks he's going out pimping again tonight, he's got another thought coming."

The guards were chuckling.

"You've got it wrong, Mom. That's not what the detective is saying," said Santa, fed up, rubbing his wrists where the handcuffs had chafed them.

"What do you mean?"

"He's saying I must be busy tonight because my name is Santa."

"Oh, I see. Ha-ha. I get it now."

The vice squad and the pimps played hide-and-seek all year long, and the worst that ever happened was somebody would have to spend a night or two in the slammer before being let go. This time was different. His case had actually been sent to the prosecutor, but the indictment was suspended because the prosecutor was too busy to deal with it. This was his third arrest this year, so clearly somebody had cooked something up to try to put the fear of God into him.

"The thing is, even the police are busy this time of year. Let's just try to make it through New Year's without any trouble, all right, Santa?"

"That might be easy for you to say, detective. But I'm not out there getting arrested because I like it. You spend ten years as a pimp, people get to know you, they even come up to you playing pachinko and slap you on the shoulder. But to get caught in the act, that's a whole nother story."

Santa's mother clunked him in the head.

"What are you talking about, you idiot? Let's go home. Detective, thank you. I won't let him make this kind of mistake again. Never. That's right."

The detective had left the guardroom even before Santa's mother was finished bowing.

As soon as they were out the front door of the police station, Santa yelled and turned up the collar of his leather jacket.

The dead ginkgo leaves at his feet fluttered up into the air.

"You've been in a nice warm place so long, you can't take this cold. Here!"

Santa's mother removed her scarf and wrapped it around his neck. He closed his mouth against the smell of her ointment, but he didn't object too strenuously.

"Maybe we should get something warm to eat."

"I'm fine. They just gave me a meal in the jail. Haven't you eaten yet?"

"Let's get some steamed buns then. Piping hot."

They could take the main road through Chinatown and be back at the apartment before the buns got cold. The neon lights were garish and hurt Santa's eyes because he had been staring at nothing but the walls.

"I just don't get it, why people think they have to have a good time just because it's Christmas. Everybody's getting all mushy all over the place."

Santa's mother clung to his arm all the way through the crowded streets of Chinatown.

"Whee! This is fun!"

"What is?"

"Oh, you don't get it. Just walking is fun. I've been sitting on a wooden floor for so long."

"Well, isn't there somebody you'd like to spend Christmas with?"

"No, that's not it. I mean, I've had nothing but women hanging all over me for ten years."

"So why don't you marry one then? What are you waiting for? I won't say anything stupid. If you had a family, I'd go live with your brother."

"You just want some other woman to have to come bail me out of jail. Like that's going to work. I don't know anybody else who would do that more than once."

His mother let out a big sigh. Her breath stank of garlic.

She seemed shorter to him. Looking down on her, he couldn't believe she was old enough for her back to be bending.

"You should go to the beauty parlor. You're starting to look like an old lady."

"If I get paid tomorrow."

The steamed bun shop was in a little alley, and there was always a line out the door. The front of the shop was decorated in scarlet and gold, and a Christmas song was playing that seemed terribly out of place.

"'Sigh-ilent nii-ight. Hoo-ooly nii-ight.' Huh. Who the hell cares? What's with all this 'Merry Christmas' crap."

His small mother stood in the line, wearing a coverall that looked too thin, scrunching her shoulders and stamping her cheap kids' sneakers.

Santa crouched at the edge of the street, puffing on a cigarette, when all of a sudden he thought of a man he had left behind in the commons room of the jail.

"Sigh-ilent nii-ight. Hoo-ooly nii-ight."

The music grew softer. Why would he be thinking about that guy?

The man's name was Kitagawa. He was fortyish, sloppy-looking, a metal worker.

"Aa-all is caa-alm, aa-all is brii-ight."

Santa recalled that when he emerged, cheerful, from the commons room, Kitagawa was singing as he stared out at the bright lights of the outside world, beyond the bars, beyond the milky glass.

"See you later," Santa said, but Kitagawa just kept looking to the side, engrossed in his singing.

No matter how he looked at it, he couldn't imagine that

Kitagawa was really a bad person.

Kitagawa had been arrested on suspicion of taking gold from his workplace and selling it on the sly to a precious metals broker. What a perfect crime.

Kitagawa had never seemed of a mind to confess the whole story. Santa couldn't think of a single good reason why he should. First of all, he was not very articulate, and second, he shrank before the gravity of the crimes he was accused of.

Among the regular prisoners in the common cell, Kitagawa was the butt of jokes.

On top of that, because of some jurisdictional issues, Kitagawa was in this jail provisionally. When his interrogation time came around, detectives from the prefectural headquarters came to escort him to a line-up where he was asked to identify other suspects. With his hands cuffed in front and tied to a rope, he looked like a peddler's monkey, and he would be brought back to his cell like that.

Once, a curious yakuza gangster asked him, "Kitagawa, how many accomplices did you have?"

Kitagawa stared up at the ceiling and bent his fingers. "Seven, I think."

This was larceny on a grand scale. With that many people involved, you could hardly call them accomplices anymore. Somebody inside the factory was slipping out the gold and selling it to a broker on the outside. Other employees at the same plant might have started doing the same thing, still completely unaware of the original crime. That didn't really make them accomplices; it was just sloppy management.

"So what kind of money are we talking about here?"

"Well, the detective told me over a hundred million yen, but I can't even imagine that much money."

"So, how about you?"

"Me...?"

"Well, take a hundred million, divide by seven, that's more than ten million each."

Kitagawa found even that figure unimaginable, and his whole body shook in denial.

"I might have gotten two hundred thousand or maybe three. I don't really remember clearly."

The others in the cell had a good laugh at that.

"Listen here, Kitagawa. You're a first offender and we're talking about two or three hundred thousand. You've been indicted and you're awaiting trial. The authorities are not that cold. The worst you'll get is short time."

An old pickpocket with thin, twisted lips turned to Santa and whispered in his ear: "Can you believe this guy? He's the perfect picture of an idiot. But somebody like you, you understand, right?"

Santa nodded. It was the prefectural police who had primary jurisdiction over Kitagawa's case, and it was the broker who was the main target of their investigation. The others, who were arrested first, were at the prefectural police station, most likely one per cell, because they wouldn't put accomplices to the same crime together in the same cell. Kitagawa must have been the last one they snapped up, and that's why he was being kept in this jail instead of that one.

In cases involving a lot of codefendants, the first ones arrested have an advantage at trial. The yen value of the crime is a matter of individual confessions, and the paperwork goes from the first to the next, down the line. So as it goes, the ones near the end of the line look much worse.

Near the end of the calendar year, if there's been a lot of crime, the police and the investigators and even the lawyers are all incredibly busy, and sometimes the paperwork gets filed all together, with hardly any time before the defense has to get started.

"I'll tell you, somebody like that shows up, weak, ignorant of the law, not too bright, and not very articulate, anybody can tell what's going to happen to him. Especially if his lawyer's some old court-appointed geezer, or even if he's not.

Before you know it, he's going to end up with two and a half years in Kurobane or Shizuoka. It's a shame."

As the old pickpocket whispered, he smiled in a way that seemed to contain less sympathy for Kitagawa than the words he was speaking.

The conversation hit a lull, and Kitagawa hugged his knees and gazed up and out the back window at the winter sky.

"Say, Kita. Where you from anyway?" Santa asked, apropos of nothing.

"A housing project near the harbor in Isogo. My dad was a longshoreman."

"Family?"

"My mom, my wife, two daughters. Sixth grade and third grade."

Without further prompting, Kitagawa started talking about his daughters.

"Round yon Virgin, mother and child. Holy infant so tender and mild."

Shielding his eyes from the bright lights of Chinatown, Santa looked up. His mother, clutching her purse, was standing in a cloud of steam.

"Mom! Buy some extra! Get ten more!"

"What in the world are you going to do with ten steamed buns?"

"Masa came by the jail and brought me some. On the way home I want to stop by and drop off something for him."

His mother took a wrinkled one thousand-yen note from him and scrunched her forehead.

"What, you're going to stop by his office? I can understand wanting to thank your brother for looking after you, but really I think you should leave well enough alone. And today of all days."

"I can't just overlook my obligations. Lady, I'll take ten of the pork buns and some of those fried dumplings. Wrap them up separately please."

In the cloud of steam, his mother exhaled a big white sigh.

"I swear, sometimes I can't tell if you're a gangster or if you're just stubborn."

At the Ishikawa-cho ticket gate, he and his mother parted ways.

"Now listen to me. I don't care if you do meet Masa, but you can't be going off playing mah-jongg or drinking the night away. It's Christmas, and your mother is going to prepare a nice meal for you and be waiting for you. You understand me? You come straight home."

Surrounded by the milling crowds, his mother just stood there endlessly, watching him leave, like a stone Jizo bodhisattva.

What am I doing? Santa thought to himself in the train car packed full of couples. Of course he had been lying about going to Takashima-cho to his brother Masa's office, but he himself could not believe he was actually heading for a housing project near the harbor in Isogo.

His thought was that this would wrap up his work for the year. Year-end and New Year's were not a good time of year for pimps in Motomachi or even Isezaki-cho, because it was a time of year people spent with their families. His mom had said tomorrow would be her payday, so if he asked her maybe she'd give him some money so he could go play pachinko.

At Isogo station, Santa counted all the money in his pocket, and he had just enough money to buy a stuffed animal. Rather than a baby doll, he bought a huge Snoopy, one he could hardly imagine anyone else would ever buy.

When he went to pay, he thought to himself, if he had this much money he wouldn't have to ask his mother for any. But still he decided the big Snoopy would be much better than the puny little Mickey Mouse.

The store clerks were laughing as they decided not to bother even trying to wrap the big Snoopy, but just to put a ribbon as big as a sunflower around its neck.

"Listen, these steamed buns are getting cold, so hurry up, okay?"

With red ribbon from the ears to one leg, the Snoopy doll looked like a present. But then there was the problem of how Santa was going to get this all the way to the housing project by the harbor.

"Could you put this on my back, so I can carry it? Like a baby?"

The customers and employees were all laughing. Santa was really embarrassed, but there was nothing he could do about it. He saw his pitiful reflection in the store window and wished they had had something else besides ribbon to use for a carrying strap.

As Santa made his way through the Christmas Eve crowds, the people walking toward him on the street gawked at him, startled.

"So, let me see. Steamed buns for the grandma, Snoopy for the two girls..."

Counting on his fingers, Santa realized that he had no gift for the wife. Never in his life had Santa given a gift to a woman he wasn't related to. With the change left over from the Snoopy he bought a potted white cyclamen. It was kind of embarrassing, but Santa knew women liked flowers.

The steamed buns were cold by now, and Santa stuck them into his jacket. He gripped the cyclamen pot in his numb fingers and carried the ridiculously large Snoopy on his back. People on the street applauded, and cars sounded their horns.

The harbor housing project was a row of old apartment buildings standing beside the red brick warehouses. Plans had been drawn up years before to tear down these buildings and replace them with high-rise condominiums, but little progress had been made because of the many elderly folks still living in the apartments.

Walking along the waterfront, he thought he was lost, but then he suddenly found himself inside the housing project. Magnificent old ginkgo trees were planted at the feet of the aging four-story apartment buildings and had shed their leaves all over the ground.

Santa tentatively asked at the police box about the house he was looking for. The young policeman, seeing Santa's get-up, found him less suspicious than laughable.

The dwellings in the project stood like dominoes, and Kitagawa's place was down at the end, facing the seawall.

"Building number eleven, in the middle, fourth floor."

Santa repeated the address to himself as he walked along. He climbed up the seawall to have a look.

The way ahead would require some courage. Should he live up to his name and say, "Merry Christmas"? But he had neither sled nor reindeer, nor a red suit. Anyone looking at him would think he was the most no-good Santa they had ever seen, and if he were to open the door, a household with no man might be particularly fearful.

Having thought for a long while, Santa turned his back on the waves coming in from the sea and descended the seawall.

He climbed the middle staircase. The Snoopy and the cyclamen pot were getting heavy. The steamed buns were by now as cold as stones.

Standing before the door, which had been repainted many times and was kind of banged-up, Santa shivered. Seeing the name Kitagawa on the door, all he could think was that that poor sucker was going to have to spend the next two and a half years in Kurobane or Shizuoka.

Santa himself was arrested many times a year, but as a mere pimp he had never actually been in a courtroom. He felt sorry for Kitagawa, who was going to have to do prison time just for taking a little bit of stuff from his workplace. As for the rest—weak, ignorant of the law, not too bright, and not very articulate—well, Santa was no better.

Try as he might, Santa could not work up the courage to knock on the door.

He wondered what Kitagawa had done with the two or three hundred thousand yen. Santa was sure it had gone for pencils and notebooks for Kitagawa's kids, underwear for his wife, or a scarf for his mother.

Santa's heart felt uncharacteristically full, and he started sobbing, right there in front of the door.

He was picturing his mother's neck, cold and uncovered by any collar or scarf as she stood at the ticket gate like a stone Jizo, wearing just her thin cleaning-lady's smock, saying goodbye to him at Ishikawa Station. Why had he not given her her scarf back?

From the dark sea a wave came crashing, and Santa felt like he was going to wet his pants.

"Who's there?" came a woman's voice from the other side of the door. Santa got nervous and ripped the ribbon from around his chest. He sat the Snoopy in the corridor, set the cyclamen pot and the steamed buns in its lap, and bounded down the narrow staircase.

He could hear the sound of the door opening. From above his head, he heard the sound of the wife's surprised voice and the happy children.

"Santa! Santa was here!"

From the darkness, Santa looked up at the fourth floor where the action was taking place.

"Santa! Thank you!"

Hearing once more the sound of the girls' shrill voices, he grew happy and climbed the seawall again.

It started to snow.

A freighter, its deck ablaze with lights, blew a Christmas whistle.

Looking up to the fourth floor of the apartment building,

Santa could see the heads of the two little girls. Santa felt the words forming at the base of his throat, but several times he swallowed them back.

I'm not Santa Claus. Your father asked me to stop by. Don't worry about the things people say. Ma'am, everything's going to be all right. Your husband will be home again before you know it.

Not one of these words he had prepared ever found its way to his voice, but Santa did finally summon up the courage to shout, in a loud voice, "Merry Christmas!"

As soon as he said it, though, he felt embarrassed and ran headlong along the seawall. The freighter's whistle echoed through the darkness of the harbor night sky, and the snow came dancing down.

Santa ran, fretting to himself about whether the real Santa Claus would be making an appearance in his sled pulled by reindeer.

Invitation from
the Orion Cinema

To: Our Esteemed Customers

Dear Sir or Madam,

On the cherry trees the blossoms are
growing plumper, and we can hardly
wait until they are at the peak of
their perfection. How are you?

Nearly a half-century has now passed
since our founding in 1950, and we feel
the Orion Cinema is now a beloved part of
the Nishijin community. Unfortunately, we
have come to the conclusion it is time for
us to close our doors.

We hope to mark this occasion with a final
thank-you show. Of course we realize you
are very busy, but we hope you can manage
to set aside time and honor us with your
presence on this special evening.

As many of our neighbors in the community
already realize, the Orion Theater has
been closed for some time due to the owner's
illness, so please note that our thank-you
event will be for one evening only.

Tomekichi Senba
Toyo Senba

Nishijin Orion Theater
Senbon-Imadegawa Sagaru Higashi
Jokyo-ku, Kyoto

The letter from the old neighborhood, which they had left long ago, included two tickets imprinted with a brocade design.

"So?" asked Yuji Miyoshi, pushing his eyeglasses back up his nose.

"What do you mean, 'so'? There's nothing more to talk about."

Yoshie didn't know what to say. What she started to say dissolved into a sigh, and she turned her eyes to the window filled with spring sunshine.

Yuji, struck anew by the beauty of her profile, felt a twinge of jealousy. He didn't want to think it was just because he was a man. When spring comes, all women are beautiful.

"I hope you're not suggesting I should go along with you." Feeling the sting of his rebuff, she turned her sad gaze away from the jostling skyscrapers.

It had been two full years since they had decided to separate. They each thought the other was just being stubborn, but as time went by, they came to an arrangement where they had lunch together once a month, religiously.

The place was always the same: the restaurant row atop the high-rise office building where he worked. Whenever they had lunch together someone never failed to notice. It was already widely whispered around the company that division chief Miyoshi had lunch on occasion with his wife.

Perhaps he was thinking too much, that because his company was making progress in its joint venture with a U.S. partner it looked like he was making a show of leading a contented family life, but Miyoshi knew that would be a requirement for securing his future career.

"You mean, you won't?" Yoshie said, sipping her coffee. He could not tear his eyes away from the red of her rouge.

"No, I'm not saying no. I may be the one being unreasonable, but as far as possible I would like to go along with your wishes. It's just that this is all so sudden."

They had bought a condominium in the center of Tokyo when the economy had been good. Little did they think it would cause their marriage to fall apart. When the economy turned sour, all they had left was a gigantic loan to pay off.

Yuji had started living in the condominium by himself, partly because it was convenient for getting to work, and partly out of stubbornness. In purchasing this particular condominium, he had given himself an insider's edge on a building he had been responsible for building, so really it had been an offense against both his wife and his company.

Before long, there was another woman. This of course led to trouble, and before you knew it they were talking about divorce, but Yuji apologized to Yoshie. He was in his mid-forties, the prime of his career, and up for an early promotion to division chief. This was not a good time for a divorce. With his employer, a major development company that had been thoroughly Americanized internally, that could be a fatal move. If such a scandal were to become public, even if the senior executives were sympathetic, he might be shipped off to an overseas branch or to some backwater in Japan. Either way, he would have no future.

"The Orion Cinema? I'm surprised to hear that place is still in business. I haven't thought about it in years."

"That's exactly why..." Yoshie said, getting into it. Her new perfume reached his nostrils, and he pulled his head back.

"We aren't even legally separated yet. It would be odd for me to go with someone else. Just imagine how happy it would make Mr. Senba and his wife if we were to go together."

"Mr. Senba and his wife are one thing. It's the other people who will be there I don't care to see. I bet they invited everybody, don't you think?"

"Oh, who cares. And besides, none of them knows a thing about what's going on with us. Yuji, just think for a minute about Mr. Senba and his wife. Once upon a time there were thirty movie theaters just in the Nishijin district, and one by one they've disappeared, but the Orion has soldiered on. Now it's the end. You can't pretend you don't care about that."

Yoshie was pressing her case like a true daughter of the old Kyoto neighborhood.

"I mean, how many years has it been after all?"

They each started counting the months and years. It had been nearly thirty years since Yuji had come to Tokyo to college, and it had been more than twenty years since Yoshie's family had packed up their weaving business and brought it to Tokyo.

"Yuji, how many times have we been back home to Kyoto?"

"Gone back home? You were still living in Kyoto the last time I went back. I haven't been in at least twenty years."

Even the phrase "back home" seemed to miss the mark. Yuji's mother had died, and his one brother and his family had moved to Osaka. Nishijin was the part of Kyoto where he had been born, but there had been nothing to draw him back there in years.

His father had been a traditional textile designer, and after his father died the family had continued to live in the same rented house. But that was it. Yuji did not feel strong ties to Nishijin. He had been to Kyoto on business many times but never felt compelled to visit the old neighborhood, where he had no living relations.

"I just don't feel like running into any of your relatives right now. I don't feel right about it in our situation."

"Relatives? I only have cousins, and there's no reason for us to go see them."

"You won't be able to just go to a movie theater right there in your old neighborhood and pretend you don't know anybody. More than likely you'll bump into your cousins right there at the Orion."

"I promise you won't have any trouble."

Yoshie was now over forty, and she must have been

feeling nostalgic for the old neighborhood. It was not that Yuji couldn't understand that. He could see though that she wouldn't have minded seeing the neighborhood where she was born at least once more, to let her distant relatives know what she'd been up to lately.

"Well, this is a fine time," Yoshie said, letting her loneliness show.

Nobody knew the details of why Yoshie's father had decided to pack up and leave Nishijin. He had grumbled 'til the day he died about what had happened to the weaving trade. Yoshie suspected that at some point he had been forced to declare bankruptcy and cut all ties to his relatives.

When they got married—two people who had both put Kyoto behind them—not one person from Kyoto was invited. At Yoshie's father's funeral, not a single person was heard to be speaking with a Kyoto accent.

Unlike Yuji's family, as the daughter of a weaving family with some standing, Yoshie still had a few ties to Nishijin. Even now, this complicated her feelings for her hometown.

"Why don't you go with your sister in Yokohama?"

"My mother wouldn't like that one bit. She doesn't like to talk about the old days. Our family left relatives, siblings, even our own graves behind. You have to understand that about her."

Yoshie's sister who lived in Yokohama and Yuji had been classmates in junior high. Once the sister came to visit his apartment and asked him if he knew of any place with part-time jobs. The family, with no strong ties in Tokyo, must have been clutching at straws.

In the course of visiting back and forth on the strength of their old friendship, Yuji had gotten interested in the sister five years younger. Anyone could see they were in love, and they got married a few years later.

"I don't want to visit the cemetery. It would be so hypocritical."

"But will you go anyway?" Yoshie said in a girlish voice.

Puffing lazily on a cigarette, Yuji looked down at the land-scape wrapped in a springtime haze.

Yuji could clearly remember the Orion Cinema in Nishi-jin. Mr. Senba and his wife managed the small theater, which faced Senbon-dori.

When Yuji was a child, that part of Nishijin had been one of the most bustling parts of Kyoto. Restaurants and movie theaters had stretched for a full kilometer from the Senbon-Imadegawa intersection all the way to Marutamachi. There were so many young men and women working in the textile shops in that area, the place always had a lively, festive atmo-sphere. Now the area near Shijo-Kawaramachi was known as "Shin-Kyogoku," or the "New Heart of Kyoto," but that part of Nishijin had been "Kyogoku," the old heart. What would it be like now?

Yuji and Yoshie had put Nishijin behind them, each for their own reasons. It might be that by now there was not a soul left there who remembered them.

Seen in that light, it seemed a miracle that the Orion Cin-ema had remained in business all this time and was only now closing its doors.

He accompanied Yoshie all the way to the entrance of the underground shopping corridor that led to the train station.

"Give me a call if it looks like you can make it. We can go and come back the same day."

"Same day? No question about it." As soon as the words had slipped out of his mouth, he wondered if he couldn't have found a warmer way to say the same thing.

There was no rational reason why the two of them had to visit their birthplace. At least not as far as concerned Yoshie, who was getting plenty of support money and who had already found a new boyfriend.

"Say, Yuji..." Yoshie said over her shoulder as she was

swept away by the crowd. "What should I do?"

Without replying, Yuji turned on his heel and started walking. The afterimage of her face lingered with him, like that of a child who had lost her way.

He did not think visiting the hometown they had each left so long ago would change a thing. With the bond between them having already grown as thin as a spider's thread, there was no reason to think such a simple, sentimental act would be able to put anything back together.

Standing between the staircase balusters, Yuji looked up at the spring light descending upon him from a great height.

Would the old Orion Cinema in Nishijin still look the same as it always had?

I should go and see, Yuji thought to himself.

·2·

"The front entrance hall used to be all white tile. There was an entrance to the left and an exit to the right, and right in the middle was the round ticket booth. Behind that stood the girl who took the tickets…"

Sitting in a private compartment on the *shinkansen*, Yoshie opened her notebook and happily started to sketch a diagram of the Orion Cinema.

"Wow, you remember it really well. I can hardly remember a thing. Do you think it was a steel-frame building?"

"No, it was all wooden. Two stories. The façade was faced to make it look like some kind of stone. Like this."

"That's right, I remember now. And there were pictures of famous stars here, like Keiichiro Akagi, and Akira Kobayashi, Mitsuo Hamada, and Izumi Ashikawa.

Yuji took the ballpoint pen from Yoshie's fingers and drew a round circle on the cinema's façade.

"Oh, that would have been a very long time ago. Was the Orion ever a first-run theater for Nikkatsu?"

"Wasn't it?"

"I think by the time I left Kyoto it wasn't a Nikkatsu theater anymore. I remember seeing the Waka Daisho series and lots of yakuza gangster movies."

"Hang on a minute. That's a crazy combination!"

"It was around that time that the movie industry was falling all to pieces. The first-run theaters weren't able to make ends meet. They were running triple features."

Once upon a time the Orion had been a first-run theater for Nikkatsu. Now that she mentioned it, by the time Yuji left for Tokyo, it may already have become a revival theater showing triple features. He had a depressing recollection of having seen some Toei yakuza triple features there.

"Old Senba and his wife have been through some hard times, I bet. Don't you remember how people in the neighborhood used to hate them? My dad used to tell me I could go to any other movie theater but the Orion."

"Yeah, in my house too. I wonder why."

"Don't you know? Senba is so much younger than his wife. That was why."

Only then did he remember. Tomekichi Senba had originally been the projectionist at the Orion. Then the owner died young, and at some point Tomekichi and the widow became intimate.

It would not be in the least surprising to learn that the gossipy little sparrows of Kyoto had whispered that the widow was a loose woman and that Senba was a usurper who had repaid good with evil. In age the two were separated by more than a full twelve years.

"This is the first time I've ever ridden in a private compartment on the *shinkansen*. I like it. You don't have to pay any mind to people all around you. We can talk as loud as we like."

When they boarded the train, he had been strangely excited. After having spent twenty years with Yoshie, why would he be feeling this fresh excitement now?

For over an hour, Yoshie had been talking continuously, hardly pausing for breath. She seemed to be in high spirits, but why would that be? It was the first time they had been alone together for some time, and she might have been afraid the conversation would turn serious. The same was true for him.

A waitress brought them coffee. During the brief pause as she added milk and sugar to hers, Yuji dove in with something he simply had to know.

"I hear you have a boyfriend."

Still gripping the spoon, her fingers stopped. Her inability to laugh off or respond to that comment was in itself an affirmative response.

"Naoya told me on the phone. He seemed shocked."

"What did he say?"

"He didn't give me any details. I think he doesn't really know much. 'Mom seems to have a boyfriend. Dad, are you okay with that? Wouldn't that be adultery?' I mean, he sees him around the house."

Anger would be the wrong move. It was Yuji who had his reasons for not getting a divorce. It may have been all of this that was going through her mind. Yoshie made no pretense of shyness. She confessed everything.

"He works at the supermarket where I've been working part-time. He's younger than me. Are you angry?"

He felt like his innards were filled with the putrid rot of anger and jealousy.

"Not really. I wonder, though, about whether he should be coming and going so freely. Naoya is in his first year of high school—he knows what goes on between men and women. You're not telling me this is a platonic relationship, are you?"

For an instant, Yoshie's gentle expression stiffened into a mask.

"Why would you think something like that? A forty-one-year-old woman and a thirty-five-year-old man?"

Yuji and Yoshie locked eyes. Yoshie's glassy eyes were saying, *You have no right to lecture me about this.*

"Don't worry though. I'm not going to marry him. Probably couldn't even if we wanted to."

"I suppose I'm the one who has to apologize."

Only then did Yoshie's lips crack a crooked smile. In the one cool corner of his seething head, Yuji reaffirmed his belief in Yoshie's beauty. Maybe that was the secret of a woman's allure.

"You don't have to apologize. I have my own little situation now."

"What is that supposed to mean?"

"Well, he has a wife and kids too. 'Double adultery.' Well, maybe not quite. One and a half anyway."

"My only point is, don't let Naoya get mixed up in this. Surely I have a right to assert myself that much."

"He only comes by to help with the garden or to fix a shutter. I need a man in the house sometimes."

"There's no need to make excuses. If you need a man's help you have Naoya."

"Are you going to try to tell me what I should and shouldn't do? We're just playing house."

"Think of what the neighbors will say."

"The only thing the neighbors are still talking about is the day that you left. But they're used to that by now. If it's Naoya you're worried about, forget it. For sex we go to a love hotel."

Without thinking, he threw his spoon at her. Yoshie's little speech was not without a touch of malice. She seemed to think she was getting him back for his own infidelity.

Alone in the compartment, they kept their silence.

On the flip side of his hatred, Yuji found himself wanting to make love to Yoshie.

"By the way, how's your girlfriend?"

The answer to this question was awkward. But he didn't have the strength to keep up appearances.

"We broke up. Her father showed up from the country-side and laid down the law. She is only twenty-six. Now that I think about it, I understand completely."

"Well, that is kind of you. Didn't you want to be together with her?"

"I can't get divorced."

"You are cold. Well, I guess I'm impressed that the ties between us are that strong."

It wasn't *ties*. This was the only way. He was carrying two mortgages. There was his position to think about. He had career ambitions. That was why divorce was impossible. That was why he couldn't marry a younger woman. Why would any woman continue seeing a man twenty years older, and one with so much baggage?

Looking long and hard at Yuji's expression, Yoshie giggled.

"So you think you've won?"

"That's not it. I was just thinking about Senba and his wife. They did the same things we're doing, and what right did anybody have to say anything about it? Actually, I think they were really admirable. No matter what the world said about them, they just carried on at the Orion."

Yuji turned away from Yoshie's gaze and looked out the train window. They must be in Shizuoka or someplace like that. Somewhere over there in the fluttering spring landscape was Matsubara.

Yuji could not bring to mind the faces of either Senba or his wife. But his memories of what they were like as people were strangely fresh.

Senba was a quiet man. If he seemed like an intellectual it was probably because children at that time idealized the notion of making a living as a projectionist. He had probably been an apprentice weaver who had worked his way up. Like all the weavers in the Nishijin district, he probably had little in the way of formal education.

He liked children. The projection room, which was in the very back of the balcony, was a kind of reserved seating for kids, who would play rock-paper-scissors to see who would be the lucky two to sit in the projection room and watch the movie through a tiny pane of glass.

As soon as he mentioned this memory, Yoshie knew right away what he was talking about.

"I remember once seeing a movie with you from the projection booth."

"That's right, I remember too. That was our first date."

"How old were we then, I wonder."

"I must have been in first or second grade, so you were either in sixth grade or the first year of junior high."

"I don't think I was in junior high yet. Once you were in junior high, you were too old to play rock-paper-scissors anymore."

He remembered something else. For whatever reason, the Orion had an unusually cheap ticket price for children. Not that it showed films that were especially for children, but these were the days before television, and lots of kids used to hang out at the movies.

It seems, for whatever reason, the Orion's bad reputation had spread to its more contemporary competitors. Not a very desirable reputation from an educational standpoint.

"Remember how tiny the window was in the projection booth? We would line up two round stools and peer out of the hole like tropical fish in an aquarium."

"It sounds so romantic when you put it that way."

In the twenty years they had lived together, Yuji had never before shared this memory with Yoshie.

There were actually two tiny windows in the second-story projection booth. At one of the two windows, on round stools, sat the two children who had won the rock-paper-scissors match. On the far side of the young Yoshie's profile was Senba, operating the projector.

Yuji thought of Senba as a rather serious man. He always felt Senba was keeping a close eye on the projector operation, using the little spotlight that illuminated just the area around his hands.

Senba wore a leather hunting cap with the brim turned to the back. His face always seemed tense, his hands were always moving, and his eyes were always following the band of light that stretched from the projector to the screen.

It was an artisan's face, a face that could be seen on all of the men in Nishijin in those days.

Yoshie gasped.

"Right here, there was a big cherry tree. You remember, don't you Yuji? In front of the show window, with the still photos. It was thi-is big."

Yoshie drew a cherry tree in the picture of the Orion Cinema whose branches reached higher than the two-story façade, gently dropping its blossoms on the tiles.

"This is it! It will be amusing to see if it's changed at all in thirty years."

In Kyoto, it would be cherry blossom time.

·3·

There is no such place as Nishijin.

When he was a child, if anyone asked where he lived, he always answered "Nishijin," and he always thought of himself as a Nishijin kid. The truth was, though, he knew "Nishijin" was a place name that could not be found on any map. This made him feel strange.

The tale was that the name went back to the Onin War, and that Yamana's western army had made its camp in the area. When Yamana came under the protection of Hideyoshi

Toyotomi, the area began to develop its long-standing reputation as a center for high-quality textiles.

If asked to describe exactly where Nishijin was, Yuji would be hard pressed to draw a line around it. The name was not official, so when he was a child the best he had was a vague idea, based on where the weaving shops were scattered here and there.

Roughly speaking, it was the area that lay to the west of Horikawa and to the north of Shimochojamachi, with Kitano Tenmangu to its west and Kuramaguchi to its north.

Depending on the fortunes and misfortunes of the textiles business, most likely older people would think of an even larger area, and younger people would think of a smaller area. For the likes of Yuji and Yoshie, though, who had been running around the back streets of Kyoto in the late 1950s and early 1960s, that rough description encompassed their birthplace, Nishijin.

The central axis of that huge weaving district was Senbon-dori, also known as Kyogoku. The only other place in Japan like it, when it came to movie theaters, would have been Tokyo's Asakusa Rokku area. Even now, if he closed his eyes, everywhere he looked he could see the colors and the lights, the bustling activity of a neighborhood that never seemed to sleep.

When they got out of the taxi at the Senbon-Imadegawa intersection, it was twilight, and it smelled of spring.

"Not a thing has changed," said Yoshie, standing dispiritedly on the street corner.

"Is that what you think? I think it's completely different."

Both views were accurate. The traditional weaving industry was at a low ebb, and so the bustling activity of the old days was no longer there, but some part of that former prosperity lingered in the old forms it left behind, and those hadn't changed.

The couple walked south along Senbon-dori.

"Even if we see somebody we know, let's not try to catch up with each and every one."

"Sure. I'll only speak if spoken to."

"How much do you plan to tell them?"

"That we met when we were children and got married. That we have a son who is in high school. That we are a picture-perfect salaryman family. That my husband works for a construction company and he's very busy, and that he hardly ever has time to come home."

"Well, you have to say we built a house in Saitama, in Higashi Tokorozawa. Perhaps they'll have heard of it. And so we bought a condominium in the city. It's a very common story in Tokyo. That we have separate living arrangements, but that we're getting along peacefully..."

"Ah, yes, peaceful. Free."

"Free to find a new girlfriend. Or boyfriend, as the case may be. This too is all too common a Tokyo story."

"I wonder..." Yoshie said, a frown replacing her smile.

"Don't you think?"

As they walked they looked up at the Nishijin sky. To the west, the spring clouds were dyed madder-red by the light of the sun setting over Nishiyama. The sunset in Tokyo never looked like this. Or was it just that they never noticed?

"Yuji. What should I do?"

Touched by the breeze of her birthplace for the first time in twenty-some years, Yoshie grew terribly sentimental. All questions of stubbornness and appearances and self-interest aside, they were really just a man and a woman.

"That's what I want to know."

"You aren't taking any responsibility. If the man doesn't decide anything, then nothing gets decided."

At that instant, Yuji remembered when the two of them had vowed their future. This was something else he had not remembered for a long time.

If Yuji was not mistaken, as the two of them had walked under the ginkgo trees in Jingu Gaien Park, the twenty-year-old Yoshie had said the exact same thing.

"*Yuji, what should I do?*"

How had he answered her then?

"*Let's get married. Be my bride. Be with me. I'll make you happy.*" He could not remember exactly how he had proposed to her. But he was certain he had not said, "That's what I want to know."

Looking up at the Nishijin evening sky, Yuji could feel himself getting older.

His wife, who had been his and his alone for so long, was being made love to by another man. In that man's strong, young arms, she was doing no more or less than what any female animal does.

Of course this was no longer the shy, modest Yoshie he knew. He could see this in the feminine charm that wafted from her demure body, her coquettish speech. His Yoshie was experiencing ecstasy in the arms of another man on a nightly basis. And her partner, a young man with a wife and children of his own, was demeaning her.

Their walk was just long enough for night to fall in Nishijin. As twilight clung like gauze to their birthplace, little by little, from somewhere in its depths, the forgotten essence of the neighborhood began to reveal itself.

Luckily, they encountered no one they knew. In all likelihood, many people, each for their own reasons, had left this part of town.

Then Yoshie grabbed Yuji's arm and came to a stop.

There, on the far side of Senbon-dori, stood the Orion Cinema, changed not one whit since their childhood.

The façade meant to make the theater look like a marble or granite building. The white-tiled entryway. The show window with its still photos from classic old movies. The round ticket booth in the center, and to its right and left the doors with their wavy glass and brass handles, open as if welcoming the couple.

The giant cherry tree was filled with blossoms at the peak of their bloom.

·4·

"It's a weeping cherry. Memory is a funny thing."

Hiding herself within the hanging, flower-covered branches, Yoshie looked up at the aging cherry tree.

"When we were little, we didn't care about things like that. Now we're old."

"Let's just say we're old enough to appreciate the beauty of things."

Yuji wondered what would happen to the cherry tree once the Orion was gone.

In his work, he had seen things like that happen all too many times. When a new building was built, there was no way to move and replant even the most magnificent cherry tree. The older and grander the tree, the greater the technical difficulty of transplanting it, and the higher the cost.

Even a client who thought of himself as very devoted to a certain tree would, at most, delay the construction a bit so he could enjoy one last blossom viewing.

There was no other possible use for a movie theater building that dated back to 1950, so most likely the building would be torn down and a modern building put up in its place. The location would be good for a condominium, a hotel, or any commercial building. Yuji didn't know who owned the land, but whoever it was would be unlikely to leave the site vacant, even if they found the idea of building distasteful.

Actually, Yuji was impressed that whoever it was had held on to the property even when land values were going through the roof.

Right next to the ticket booth stood a sign: FINAL THANK-YOU SHOW: TODAY ONLY. There were hardly any people worth noticing though. The six thirty start time was not that far off, but there were hardly any guests.

Inside the box of the round ticket booth, someone stood up. It was Tomekichi Senba.

"Look, it's Senba. I'm sure of it. That's Senba."

That Mr. Senba would be there was really no surprise at all, but Yoshie was acting as if it were some odd coincidence.

"Hello, Mr. Senba. It's been a long time." Yoshie bowed politely, and Senba, flustered, opened the small side door at his feet and came out.

He stood on the tiles, which were covered with cherry blossoms just as Yoshie had drawn them in the picture, and stood at attention like a soldier. He pushed his old-fashioned eyeglass frames up his nose and bowed deeply.

"Do you know who I am?" Yuji asked, walking up close to him.

"I know you, I do. You're old Miyoshi's Yuji. And so this must be…" he continued, but his confidence faded. "If I'm not mistaken, you would be the younger daughter from the Senju-ya shop. What was your name?"

"Yoshie. I'm so glad you remember me."

"That's it, Yoshie! Your older sister is Mitsue, and so you're Yoshie. Thank you so much for coming. I heard you two got married, and you live in Tokyo. You must be very happy."

Senba looked them over carefully.

Had he always been that small? He was the perfect image of the owner of a movie theater on its very last day. His hair was white and long. He wore a turtleneck sweater. Everything about him said Orion Cinema, as if he had been torn from the pages of a storybook.

"My, how grown up you are. And you do look so happy. Any children?"

"One son, now in high school. We are just a stereotypical salaryman family. My husband is always so busy with his job at the construction company, he hardly ever comes home."

The very phrases they had been joking about before now came tumbling out of Yoshie's mouth. When she finished speaking, the two of them exchanged glances and laughed.

"Yeah, it's kind of far from our house to my office, so we bought a condominium in the city. We have separate living arrangements, but we're getting along peacefully."

Still laughing, Yoshie went on. "This kind of thing goes on all the time in Tokyo. It's nice to have so much freedom."

Just as it seemed he was about to say more, Yuji stopped himself.

Senba was looking blankly at the talkative couple.

"Ah, yes, well, that's all very nice. Childhood sweethearts, that's sweet."

Senba had grown very old, but he still wore the very same eyeglasses as before, Yuji noticed. Thick black frames, one hinge still broken, wrapped thickly with cellophane tape.

Just as he noticed those eyeglasses, an unbidden tear welled up in his eye. Even way back when, the hinge of Senba's eyeglasses had been wrapped with cellophane tape.

"How's your wife? Is she well?" Yoshie asked.

"Well, to tell the truth, she's been in the university hospital for quite some time now. I think everybody knows by now, but the fact is she's eighty-five years old. I'm seventy myself, and I'm still doing all right, but we've been managing this little place just the two of us all these years. She's getting kind of senile, and I've been doing my best to look after her, but we just can't go on like this."

Senba's eyelids fluttered as he spoke.

Which was his way of saying that was why they had to close the place.

Yuji handed him a business card, and Senba looked surprised.

"I...I don't know what to say."

"Is something wrong?"

"This is some coincidence. We've been giving this place

its last rites and decided to build a new building, and we hired your company to do it."

Given the size of Yuji's company, this was no real surprise, but still he got all choked up.

"Your main office in Kyoto is over there on Karasuma. There's a man named Ogura there, a section chief, and he's been doing a lot for us. You know him?"

Yuji didn't know any section chief named Ogura. To avoid causing any misunderstanding, he had to be careful about what he said next.

"Well, that is quite a coincidence. Kansai is not part of my territory, and I don't know Ogura. My trip here today is purely personal."

As he spoke, Yuji's voice grew fainter because he could now see exactly how the Orion Cinema would be destroyed.

When land prices had been going through the roof, Yuji knew that his company's Kyoto office had done everything in its power to buy up as much land as possible. Clearly Senba had paid no attention to their exorbitant offers, and he had kept the lights on at the Orion Cinema. Now that the real estate boom was over, the theater owner was an old man, and it was not hard to imagine how different the offer would be.

"I'm sure he's only looking out for himself. I'm sorry if he's giving you a hard time."

"Don't be ridiculous. Mr. Ogura has been very good to me. He's taken care of my wife's funeral arrangements, so I don't have to worry about anything. He bought me a condominium near Ichijoji. That's closer to the hospital. That way I can look after the Mrs., and just live a life of leisure...I wonder what's going on here tonight, though. Nobody at all has shown up. Maybe we should just get started."

Senba looked up and down the street with lonesome eyes, then stepped inside the darkened cinema.

"Mr. Senba, how much is admission?" Yoshie asked from behind him.

"Oh don't worry about that. What would I do with your money anyway? For fifty years the good people of Nishijin have fed me well, and hard work has been my good fortune. Don't even think about it. To the very end, I've been able to show my customers some enjoyment. I have no regrets, and neither does this theater. I want to thank you all very much."

The theater was spic-and-span. The carpet had been vacuumed so there was not a single speck of dust, and the brass rail up the stairs was gleaming. At the landing at the bottom of the stairs, Yoshie stood stock still, as if she had grown roots.

"Is something wrong, Yoshie?" Senba asked.

Looking down at her feet and covering her mouth, Yoshie finally said, "Right here, this is where we used to play rock-paper-scissors. The ones who wanted to watch from the projection booth."

Looking up at Yuji, her eyes were dazzling. Yuji remembered as if it were yesterday the day he won the game and bounded up these very stairs. Taking Yoshie's hand in his now, they climbed the stairs together.

The Orion Cinema was the one place their parents had told them never to go. But of all the thirty movie theaters standing in a row, the Orion was the one they most wanted to go to. Why was that? It wasn't because the admission was lower. It wasn't because they liked the Nikkatsu teenager movies. The Orion simply always had a kind embrace for the children of the home workers of Nishijin, who were not always able to look after their own children all the time.

It may be that Yoshie was only now realizing this for the very first time.

"Why is the Orion so nice?" So saying, Yoshie crouched down and stroked the grimy carpet lovingly. "My father, my mother, every grown-up I knew said the same thing. 'Don't go to the Orion. It's a crappy place, a dump, don't go there. The lady is a tramp, and that other guy is a usurper who shows no respect for the master. Don't go there.' That's what they used to say."

"Enough, Yoshie," Yuji scolded.

As soon as he raised his voice he felt a lump in his chest. But not because of Yoshie.

Yuji had thought for a long time Nishijin was no longer part of his life. He thought of Nishijin as a place of narrow backstreets and narrow-minded artisans, where malicious gossip just went on and on with no escape. He couldn't stand that. He had packed up and left for Tokyo and never wasted another thought on the old neighborhood. He felt no nostalgia or homesickness. It was a clean break. For twenty years he had had a Nishijin woman at his side, but he had failed to keep that love alive.

Through all of that, the projector lights had stayed on at the Orion Cinema, and life had gone on on Senbon-dori.

"Really? Is that what everybody said about us?" Senba asked as he slowly climbed the steps to the second floor, looking down at the pair who had stopped in the middle. How sad his eyes were.

"I never knew that. How stupid of me."

"How stupid of you too," Yuji reprimanded Yoshie again.

The small chandelier cast the aging projectionist in shadow.

"Listen here, Yuji, Yoshie. Let me tell you my side of the story. Don't ever say that again. I don't care if you believe me or not, I never stole anything from anybody. I swear to God."

Yoshie stood up and looked up at Senba.

"What do you mean?"

"I came here as an apprentice, and the old man taught me everything, to the last detail. Then he got lung disease, and he had to give up, and the old guy took me by the hand and he said, 'Tome, don't let the shop shut down. Don't let go of the theater. You won't see Yujiro's photograph on just any old theater. Any flimsy old building can be a first-run Nikkatsu theater, but sooner or later the floor's going to collapse. The Orion is the only place in Nishijin where the weavers and their kids can come to see Yujiro and Akira Kobayashi. You hear me? Don't let it go! I'm begging you.' That's what the old man said."

From his back pocket, Senba pulled out his folded-up hunting cap. In the spacious second-story hall, Senba approached the projection booth one step at a time, as if he were carving them.

"Would you care to sit in one of the mezzanine boxes?"

"No, I want to sit over *there*," Yuji said, pointing to a steel ladder attached to the wall of the theater.

"You mean the projection booth?"

"That's right. It always was my favorite seat. Isn't that right, Yoshie? All right with you?"

Yoshie didn't answer. She just kept walking, head down, with a troubled look on her face.

"Mr. Senba, can I ask you a question?"

"And what might that be?"

"Do you mean to say there has never been anything between you and the lady of the house?"

Senba laughed out loud.

"I thought I explained that already."

"Huh?"

"She wrote me into her family register, and so I became her husband. We are officially man and wife. Now, if nothing ever happened between man and wife, that would be an offense against the heavens. She was still young then. That's the end of my little speech. Let's watch the movie."

Senba climbed agilely up the ladder and waved a welcome to them from the door of the projection room, just as he had when they were children.

"We're going to get started. Yuji, Yoshie, come on up here."

·5·

From the tiny window of the projection room, Yuji looked down at the house seats.

In a mezzanine box near the front, there was a young couple, and on the main level there were four or five other people sitting here and there. That was it. In the blind spot in the back there was probably no one at all. In the good old days, the hall was always filled with heads, even in the aisles and all along the walls. Yuji remembered this as if in a dream.

The air in the theater was the cleanest it had ever been.

"Was this place always this small?" Yoshie wondered aloud as she sat on the round seat.

"It's not that the theater is small. We've just gotten bigger."

Even the projection room seemed to have been much larger back in the day.

"I have to welcome the public," Senba said, clearing his throat and reaching for the ancient microphone.

"We would like to thank you for your visit to the Orion Cinema today, on the occasion of our final thank-you event. What I always really wanted, if I could, was to die right here in this projection room with the film still rolling, but all I can manage is this modest program. My sincere apologies."

The whole time he spoke, Senba faced the screen, standing rigidly at attention.

"My predecessor opened this theater in April 1950. Ever since then, I have worked hard, always with the commitment that the lights should never go out in the movie houses of Nishijin. That's right. Even so, I'm getting old now, and my eyes, which are so vital to this work, aren't what they used to be. I really did want to die showing a movie, but my doctor has convinced me it's time to give up, and my wife, well she's not doing so well…"

Senba dabbed at his eyes with the sleeve of his sweater, like a child.

"Mr. Senba, hang in there," Yoshie said, standing up and placing her hand on his shoulder.

"Sorry to bother you with these things, but there was a lot that happened. This theater, and the movies, are the only things my wife and I know anything about, and this was the only way we knew to make a living, and we always did the best we could after our own fashion. Sometimes we barely had enough to put food on the table. Sometimes we couldn't afford the payments for the films. Sometimes the bean-paste buns from the snack counter were all we had to eat, three meals a day. Like every other theater in the country, it even entered our minds to show porn. But if we did that we wouldn't be able to let the kids into the theater. If all the old movie theaters in Nishijin started showing porn, we would be the laughingstock of the entire city, and I wouldn't be able to face my ancestors. Somehow we've been able to get by, by the skin of our teeth, as a revival theater. Having to shut down the Orion Cinema still seems to me like I'm breaking my promise never to get rid of the place. Life is precious, and I feel like I'm somehow doing harm to the movies themselves. As a man, as a person, as someone at the bottom rung of the film profession, I am ashamed, but no matter what anyone says there is nothing more I can do. Now I'm standing here just making excuses. You must forgive me. And now, without further ado, our final picture. I hope you enjoy it. This is a film of great sentimental value to me. It is the first film I ever showed on the Orion Cinema screen after my wife and I got together. Even now my wife..."

The aging projectionist hung his head and held the mic behind his back, his shoulders heaving, lips tightening, and cried.

"This morning, when I went to see her in the hospital, before I even said a word she was talking about how much she loved this movie. It was the first film we showed together here at the Orion Cinema, and it made us so happy. The 1957 film *Sun in the Last Days of the Shogunate*, by director Yuzo Kawashima, with a script by assistant director Shohei Imamura. Starring Frankie Sakai, Sachiko Hidari, Yoko Minamida, Yujiro Ishihara, and Izumi Arakawa. The running time is 110 minutes. Thank you for coming today. Thank you very much."

From the level below, they could hear quiet but sincere applause.

Senba bowed deeply, first facing the screen and then in the direction of the projector. Then he stiffened his thumb to push the button on the wall.

The bell signaled the opening of the curtain. Senba turned his hat around the other way and gave a meaningful look to Yuji and Yoshie.

"Pardon me, but would you mind flipping that switch right there?"

Slowly Yuji pulled down the switch that controlled the house lights. Darkness fell.

"I'm sorry you had to witness that inappropriate monologue. The guy looking after the movie house has never cried before. Today of all days, for this to happen..."

Trying to smile, Yuji held his breath.

In the small circle of light from the spotlight, Senba stood like a statue, pressing to his chest a single photograph.

"The truth is, my wife died this morning, and that's why this happened today of all days. And the wake...you'll have to pardon me."

Senba set the photograph beside the projector lens.

"Now you can rest easy. You must be very tired. Let's watch the film together, you and I."

The brilliant band of light cut through the darkness.

The dazzling spectacle of the cherry tree in full bloom in front of the Orion Cinema was unforgettable.

The full moon hung like a paper cutout in the sky above Senbon-dori.

Yuji and Yoshie told Senba they wanted to stay for the funeral, but he declined politely, with a smile.

"Thank you so much, but you have already mourned enough. The Orion Cinema itself is her casket, and the blossoming of the cherry tree was her floral offering. Who could ask for anything more?"

Looking up at the cherry blossoms now fluttering down, Yoshie said, "Yeah, who could ask for more than this."

The meaning of these words struck him, and Yuji bit down with his back teeth.

While they waited for a taxi, Yuji and Yoshie turned to look back one last time at the Orion Cinema's white façade, now wrapped in cherry blossoms.

"It was a good movie, wasn't it? Yuzo Kawashima and Frankie Sakai are both dead, but they were real geniuses, don't you think? Are you really going all the way back to Tokyo tonight?"

They had tickets for the last train.

"Well, you know how it is. There's a lot going on. If we have a chance we'd like to come back soon."

"I see, is that so? Well, the theater won't be here anymore, and I'll be just an old man. No reason to come see me. Let's just say this is 'The End.'"

Smiling, Senba reached his hand through the taxi window.

"Well then, goodbye, goodbye. You've become such a success, I'm sure you've had your troubles too. You will accomplish great things if you try. Thank you so much for coming all the way here tonight."

As the car drove away down Senbon-dori, Senba stood like a spirit in front of the Orion Cinema, surrounded by falling cherry blossoms, his head bowed for as long as he remained in sight.

Looking out the car windows as their old neighborhood passed before them, Yoshie began to quietly sing a half-forgotten song.

"Yuji, what are we going to do about us?" she said, lapsing into Kyoto dialect. She herself couldn't believe she had said this, and she pressed her hand against her lips.

"Enough already," Yuji said, also in Kyoto dialect, and asked the driver to stop.

"Driver, I'm sorry but I've changed my mind. Turn left on Marutamachi and take us to the Miyako Hotel. I'm too tired to go all the way back to Tokyo."

The full moon disappeared behind a cloud, and a spring rain began to fall on Nishijin. Gazing at his wife's silent profile, Yuji was looking forward to a walk in the rain tomorrow.

Instead of an Afterword

·The Volume of Miracles·

Poppoya (*The Stationmaster*) was first published in April 1997. It was my first collection of short stories.

It is customary for paperback books to be marketed with a catchphrase that summarizes the theme. For the first edition of this book, the phrase on the cover was,

"Miracles so simple, they could happen to you."

Which more or less said that this was a collection of short stories with a miracle motif.

At first I felt this to be a rather embarrassing idea, but in the end I concluded it was a good tagline. It would make me happy if people were to read the eight stories in this book and feel that some small miracle had taken place in their hearts.

Personally, I have no fundamental belief in divinity received from gods and buddhas or through pious actions. Divination, fate, spiritual beings, or anything that cannot be explained scientifically are all things I do not believe in. Lacking in great dreams, I was unworthy of becoming a writer, but I was able to become one through sheer force of will. In the end I have lived my life without God or Buddha, and there's nothing that can be done about it.

I did believe, however, in miracles, the kind that can be evinced by unrelenting effort or sincere anguish. Or at the very least I believed in miraculous consequences.

One such miracle is the very fact that I, who never showed any sign of anything resembling talent, am now a recognized, professional writer. It is as if a youth who dreamed of soaring through the vast sky found he had become a bird simply by flapping his arms around.

I knew these kinds of inner miracles could happen to anyone.

For about a year and a half starting in 1994, I was busy writing the longer work *Soukyuu no Subaru* (蒼穹の昴).

Once that manuscript was finished, I felt compelled to write a lot of shorter pieces, a fact that reflects my background as a former member of Japan's Self-Defense Forces. That is to say, having completed one course of action I had built up certain muscles, but this had allowed other muscles to wither at the same time. So the next thing I had to do was focus on replenishing those parts, to restore the balance of my strengths.

One thing one forgets when writing a longer work of fiction is the sharpness of thought that goes into shorter works. Sentences with no fat. Clear focus of thought and theme.

Put plainly, this is analogous to taking a body grown torpid from having run marathons and restoring its strength by repeatedly running short-distance intervals.

After finishing the long manuscript in September, I wrote two short stories, which were first published in the magazines *Shosetsu Subaru* and *All Yomimono*. Those were "The Stationmaster" and "Devil," included in this volume.

Until that time, I had thought of myself as more suited for writing longer works, and I had little experience writing shorter fiction. After submitting these two stories to the respective editors, my mental state was that of a sprinter, panting and unable to take my eyes off my watch.

My interest in taking on the challenge of short fiction was steeled, and at the same time, I found new opportunities for testing my own qualifications. The day I handed those two stories to the editors was longer and more depressing than the later day when I was considered for the Naoki Prize.

Happily, those two stories found far better treatment than they deserved and were published in the November 1995 issues of the magazines *Shosetsu Subaru* and *All Yomimono.*

Even though "The Stationmaster" and "Devil" were written during the exact same period of my life, the two stories could hardly be more different.

"The Stationmaster" is written in a third-person omniscient voice, and many of the details of the story are provided through dialogue.

"Devil" is written in a first-person limited voice, and the structure of the text is quite plain and hard.

I made the decision to use these different methods for these two stories quite deliberately. I could not tell which method would work better for me, so I was experimenting with two contrasting methods. Rereading these stories now, I think I was quite naïve at the time.

When I was forty-two I was still driving trucks at night, trying to figure out how to go faster; nothing had changed from when I was nineteen.

"Love Letter" is a description of some events that actually occurred in my personal sphere at a time when I was living an unsavory life. They say truth is stranger than fiction, and this is a story that demonstrates that. I am keenly aware that this was a story I did not seek out but was thrust upon me. It took a circuitous route, but in the end I was able to write a story like this, and I feel strangely comfortable with that.

"In Tsunohazu" is the story of my own wretched childhood. Of course some of the details have been changed, but by and large it is a true story.

Amid my disappointment when I was at first rejected for the Naoki Prize, and pressed by a magazine deadline, I submitted a manuscript to my editor that I was not fully satisfied with, with the words, "This is the only kind of thing I could write." Rereading that story now, I think I could only have written it at that time. In other words, if *Soukyuu no Subaru* had not been rejected for the Naoki Prize, I would never have been able to write "In Tsunohazu."

I needed to take an experience I felt I could not write about and turn it into something I couldn't *not* write about.

"Kyara" is my own memorial to half my life. I worked for a long time in the fashion industry, and the whole time I wrote stories I could never sell. Even now if I leave the house, I am more likely to visit a lady's boutique than a bookstore. If I cast a glance at a woman leaving the store as I enter, it is not an amorous impulse; I am checking out her fashion sense based on long years of habit.

Whenever I reread the first line of "The Festival of Lanterns," I get all choked up, based on pure personal emotion. All of the personal experiences that went into "Devil" and "In Tsunohazu" are summed up in this one sentence. At the end, when Chieko comes to the sudden realization that she wants to have a child, the thought comes "rising up within her like a flame from deep inside her chest." The energy that makes me continue to write stories is exactly like that.

The story "No-Good Santa" contains a secret. In the process of compiling these short stories, I wanted to write a story containing the image of myself, as I am. The same way Michelangelo quietly included his self-portrait in the Sistine Chapel ceiling. Readers may find this surprising, but people who know me burst out laughing in recognition when they first read this short-short story, because Santa Kashiwagi *is* me.

"Invitation from the Orion Cinema" may be the story that says the most about me.

My memory of writing this is that I did it fluidly without thinking too much. It's just a story that seems fitting in my hand, a perfect expression of what it is that I do. If some foreigner, a stranger to me, were to ask me what my stories were like, I might hand him this one instead of a business card.

I have no way of knowing if this story collection, *The Stationmaster*, has caused any miracles to happen for my readers as the catchphrase promised.

This book, however, has caused miracles for me, who always wanted so badly to be a writer.

Someday, when my time comes, it is my dream to collapse on a snow-covered train platform like the obstinate old stationmaster himself, with my whistle in my lips and my flag in hand.

– Jiro Asada

Jan

The translator wishes to
thank Sayuri Kingsbury
for her assistance.

A NOTE ON THE TYPE

Closely modeled on Goudy Old Style, Goudy Catalogue was designed by Morris Fuller Benton in 1919. Based on the original types of beloved American book and type designer Frederic W. Goudy, this version has the Old Style feel and design characteristics of his original (which was one of Goudy's most widely used fonts and later adapted for the University of California Press in 1938), but is slightly heavier and just a hair wider.